Vignettes & Postcards

Writings From the Evening Writing Workshop at Shakespeare and Company Bookstore, Paris Original Edition (Fall 2011)

Foreword Book of the Year Finalist

Next Generation Indie Book Award Winner

Readers' Favorite Silver Award

Readers' Favorite 5-Star Award

International Book Award Finalist

USA Book News Best Book Award Finalist

Anderbo Top Finalist Book

Paris Book Festival, Honorable Mention

New York Book Festival, Honorable Mention

San Francisco Book Festival, Honorable Mention

SPECIAL NEW EDITION

Vignettes
&
Postcards
From Paris

SPECIAL NEW EDITION

Vignettes
&
Postcards
From Paris

EDITORS
ERIN BYRNE
ANNA POOK

REPUTATION BOOKS

VIGNETTES & POSTCARDS FROM PARIS

Published by Reputation Books, LLC
reputationbooksllccom

Book Design: Lisa Abellera
Photographs © William Curtis Rolf and Sabine Dundure
Sketches © Candace Rose Rardon and Colette Hannahan

ISBN 978-09852672-0-9 (paperback)

ISBN 978-0-9852672-3-0 (e-book)

Reputation Books Edition: August 2016

10 9 8 7 6 5 4 3 2 1

Reputation Books

In memory of George Whitman,
literary monarch and conjurer of dreams
1913-2011

We must never be afraid to go too far, for the truth lies beyond.
—Marcel Proust

You risk tears if you let yourself be tamed.
—Antoine de Saint-Exupéry, *The Little Prince*

Contents

Illuminations

Portraits

Vignettes & Postcards
Writings From the Evening Writing Workshop at Shakespeare and Company Bookstore, Paris Original Edition (Fall 2011)

Visions

Memory

Mystery

Odes

Nouveau

If a little dreaming is dangerous, the cure for it is not to dream less, but to dream more, to dream all the time.
                              —Marcel Proust, *Within a Budding Grove*

Nouveau

Erin Byrne

T HERE'S A NEW PLACE IN P ARIS where you can get a piece
of real lemon pie and a café crème so tantalizing it will melt
your inhibitions. Inside this once-medieval space are stacks of
books on shelves, and small tables packed with people writing,
debating, or dreamily gazing out the window, *passez les temps.*
It's the new café next to Shakespeare and Company, and
although he's been gone for five years, it's the one thing George
Whitman always felt was missing from his haven of books.
Sylvia has made it light and pretty, with a white façade and
brightly colored chairs, but it matches the care-worn ambiance
of the bookshop perfectly, as if a sprinkling of cinnamon on top
of a Cappuccino.

Even the café's motto, "Open door, open books, open mind,
open heart," goes with the old one in the shop, surrounded by

the vivid spines of books: "Be not inhospitable to strangers, lest they be angels in disguise."

Our *nouveau* section to this beloved, award-winning anthology of writings from there adds extra spice in the same way. We have included twenty-one new stories and poems that bring you to Paris before escorting you into Shakespeare and Company for the cherished original ones.

Don George flings wide the shutters of his heart to *la bonne vie*, and Marcia DeSanctis pats a vacant seat next to her on a velvet banquette in Le Grand Véfour, where Napoléon and Josephine once nestled. We set out with Georgia Hesse to meander markets and so much more. Jayme Moye takes us out into twilit Paris, where streetlamps illuminate footsteps on cobblestones, and laughter bursts out of bistro doors as they swing open. We open a book of Paul Valéry's poems, and Billy Collins pulls one out by the hand to introduce her. The top-hatted SpokenWord poets of Paris, writing in the imaginative style emblematic of Paris itself, offer our minds a holiday, with Alberto Rigettini's Phantom of the Opéra Station, David Sirois' odes to the plentiful pigeons of Paris, and David Barnes' discovery in Père Lachaise. Catherine Karnow details her long engagement with Paris, and Gonzague Pichelin presents a Portrait of a Bookstore as an Old Man. William Curtis Rolf's exquisite images and Candace Rose Rardon's intricate sketches offer new vistas of Paris, while Colette Hannahan's images delight the eye.

So, you see, this new edition, *Vignettes & Postcards from Paris,* sashays us around the city, then tiptoes us up the rickety stairs. The mystique is still there—the ghost of Walt Whitman, the Mirror of Love, Sylvia Plath's pathos, and scales resounding from the old piano—resonating in the original stories which have never ceased sparking with inspiration and heart, and invite us again to curl up on a cushion and sink into this book.

Afterwards, let's stop in next door for a Flapjack Kerouac or a slice of George's Lemon Pie. Before you lift the steamy cup to your lips, don't forget to shake in a little shush of cinnamon.

—Erin Byrne
January, 2016

La Bonne Vie

Everything belongs to those who can appreciate it.

—André Gide

La Bonne Vie in Paris

Don George

I FIRST MOVED TO PARIS AS a French literature undergraduate on a Princeton summer work-abroad program. Living with an aristocratic French family in shabby 16th-arrondissement splendor, I sipped the simultaneous thrills of inhabiting the past, surrounded by 18th-century family portraits, armoires, and settees, and rewriting the present in a foreign tongue. My providential presence provided the twentysomething heir of the family and his exuberant fiancée with the perfect excuse to concoct elaborate picnics and parties, and by the middle of the summer, I had a new answer when people asked me what I was doing in Paris: *"J'étudie la bonne vie française,"* I'd say—I'm studying the good life, French style.

When I moved back for a second summer on the same program, everything was different. This time I had the confidence to tackle the city on my own, and having just graduated,

I felt exhilaratingly untethered; life stretched before me like a grand boulevard of possibilities, all intriguing alleys and archways. After a withering week looking for lodging, I discovered a dream place on the fashionable rue de Rivoli, just opposite the glorious green Jardin des Tuileries. I was supposed to stay confined to the former maid's rooms in the interior of this sprawling apartment, but after a few days the owners left for a month on the Mediterranean, and that evening I found a way to unlock the door into the main salon. Towering French windows opened onto the Tuileries deepening into twilight, and as I gazed in wonder, the summer Ferris wheel's lights began to blink like fireflies and the majestic sounds of an open-air orchestra swelled on the breeze.

Hungry in a way I'd never been before, I gorged on Paris. I watched Molière at the Comédie Française and the Ballet Béjart in the park; I idled among the secondhand shelves at Shakespeare and Co., eavesdropping on poets and poseurs; I immersed myself in Manet and Monet in the Musée d'Orsay; bobbed on a *bateau mouche* along the Seine; got lost in the ancient alleys of Montmartre and the Marais; stood stunned in stained-glass silence in Notre-Dame; savored the open-air theater from a sidewalk café on the Champs-Élysées; conjured Hemingway on rue Descartes and Les Deux Magots café; and found my own dinner table at a boudoir-size bistro around the corner from my apartment, where I knew I'd arrived when the owner brought me my *bifteck-frites* and demi-carafe of house red wine without a word.

One evening I was walking home from work and came upon two college students from Alabama who were clearly lost. I helped the young women find their way back to their hotel, which turned out to be the hallowed Ritz. In gratitude their parents invited me to join them the next two nights, first for the famous duck dinner at the opulent Tour d'Argent—"one of the most expensive restaurants in Paris," my envious colleagues told me the next day—and then for the flashy, fleshy fête at the Moulin Rouge, which somehow led to a Champagne-fueled soirée back at the Ritz, until the bells rang in the rosy dawn.

It was that kind of summer. I fell in love a few times, but of course, my real love was for Paris. I would wander its streets inebriated with the inexpressibly elegant avenues and façades, the arching bridges and graceful streetlamps, the laughter spilling out of bistros and bars, the musicians in the métro, the soft-lit windows in the grand apartments on the Île Saint-Louis, where I yearned to join the soigné citizens and their sophisticated repartee.

One morning halfway through my stay, I took my apartment building's rickety old filigreed elevator as usual from the fifth floor to the hushed shade of the ground-floor entryway, then stepped through the massive wooden doors into the street—and stopped. All around me people were speaking French, wearing French, acting French. Shrugging their shoulders and twirling their scarves and drinking their cafés crèmes, calling out "*Bonjour, monsieur-dame*" and paying for *Le Monde* or *Le Nouvel Observateur* with francs and stepping importantly around me and staring straight into my eyes and subtly smiling in a way that only the French do.

Until that summer, I had spent most of my life in classrooms, and I was planning after that European detour to spend most of the rest of my life in classrooms. Suddenly it struck me: This was the classroom. Not the musty, ivy-draped halls in which I had spent the previous four years. This world of wide boulevards and centuries-old buildings and six-table sawdust restaurants and glasses of *vin ordinaire* and poetry readings in cramped second-floor bookshops and mysterious women smiling at you so that your heart leaped and you walked for hours restless under the plane trees by the Seine. This was the classroom.

In that moment, the seed of my future sprouted. Rather than write about literature, I would write about life in the world, beginning with a graduate course in *la bonne vie française.*

Twenty Years and Counting

On the things we set in motion

Marcia DeSanctis

Since 1784, Le Grand Véfour has occupied the northwest corner of the Jardins du Palais Royal in Paris. The restaurant seems forever married to the words "venerable institution" because of the roster of French luminaries—from Napoléon to Victor Hugo to Jean-Paul Sartre—who have warmed its velvet banquettes over the years. And then there's me. One fall afternoon twenty years ago, I had my wedding dinner there. Just weeks later, a young Savoyard chef named Guy Martin was plucked from the Hotel Château de Divonne in the tiny Lake Geneva spa town of Divonnes-les-Bains to lead Le Grand Véfour into the twenty-first century. I had never met Guy Martin, but this year, at both of our two-decade marks, I wondered if there might be parallels between the life of a restaurant and the course of a marriage. So I returned to Le Grand Véfour to raise a glass to history—France's, the restaurant's, and my own.

I first ate at Le Grand Véfour in the summer of 1983 with a sporty count named Nicolas who squired me around Paris in a Fiat Spider, but whose diminished circumstances became obvious when the bill arrived. He was a couple hundred francs short. But what did I care who paid the check? Champagne was coursing through our veins and the restaurant's gilded opulence gave us the sensation that we were tucked inside a fancy chocolate box. Despite its age, Le Grand Véfour had the order and polish of something new and, for me, uncharted. Glass panels lined the dining room, along with portraits of fleshy, bare-breasted goddesses bearing peaches or colored ices—paintings two hundred years old, but with hues and sentiments as fresh as that July morning. All around me, the thrill of seduction mingled with the tranquility of permanence.

The scent of tarragon wafted up from my lamb chops, and cassis ice cream added another layer of pleasure, which—along with Nicolas' hand intermittently grazing my thigh under the table—heightened the anticipation in all my senses. The bubbly, his lips on my bare shoulder, a warm summer night—Le Grand Véfour was promise itself and the pure essence of Paris. I never forgot it.

Eight years later I was back, living in Paris and working as a journalist, traveling for stories in Eastern Europe and the Middle East. When I got engaged to Mark, an American sculptor, there seemed no question that we would forego the big to-do stateside and get married in the city we now called home. He had bought my engagement ring—a gorgeous and well-worn platinum, diamond, and sapphire band—at an upscale pawnshop on the rue de Turenne, for 1,200 francs, or about $200 at the time. Our rented apartment had a fancy Marais address, but I'd spent the better part of the previous year steaming off the stained brown wallpaper that covered every inch of the place, substituting the bare light bulbs on the ceiling with fixtures from the market at Clignancourt, and hiding the prewar linoleum under carpets I bought at *souks* from Istanbul to Fez.

In France, no one cared where we went to college or what our fathers did back home. We worked hard, scraped by, consorted with journalists and artists, and weren't on any regular family dole that propped up our lifestyle. Still, I was the youngest of four unmarried daughters, so my parents were eager to foot the bill for whatever I chose for the fifty people we planned to invite—family, a few good friends from the States and, mostly, those who comprised our life in France.

I had already lived in Paris long enough to dress the part, but some other things remained difficult for a young American woman. Like finding a wedding venue. I aimed high, but Paris was shutting me out. I inquired at what seemed like the city's entire varsity restaurant line-up: L'Orangerie and L'Amboiserie, Taillevent and Maison Blanche. In each dining room, the gatekeeper shook his head, topped it off with a puckered expression of Gallic scorn, and sent me packing. They seemed to be telling me what I suspected: We had no business getting married in such a place. Yankee, go home.

I hadn't dared approach Le Grand Véfour; it was considered a sanctum, impenetrable and holy, despite a perceived decline I'd read about following the recent death of its chef of thirty-six years. But one day, while getting a haircut at a salon in the Galerie Vivienne, I realized I was a stone's throw from the restaurant.

"Your hair looks very sad," my *coiffeuse*, Monique, told me flatly, referring to my brunette locks.

"Really?" I asked. Two hours later I walked out a blonde, and not a classy-looking one.

Maybe it was the hair that made me lose my guile, because something marched me straight over to Le Grand Véfour. I stopped to read the placard in memory of Colette, who had lived upstairs and who, at the end of her life, was carried down each day for lunch at her lavish personal canteen. I turned the corner on the rue de Beaujolais and walked inside, where I was greeted by an imposing woman with a spray of silk ruffles at her neck.

"Hello," I said. "I'm getting married on September 7th at the *mairie* of the 3rd arrondissement, and afterwards, I would like to have my dinner here."

To my astonishment, her face lit up.

"I'm Madame Ruggieri," she said. "Congratulations. We would be delighted to host your celebration."

—◦◦◦—

When our wedding party arrived at Le Grand Véfour on an unusually sultry Saturday in September, waiters greeted us beneath the colonnade with flutes of pink Champagne on silver trays. At the time, the wine giant Taittinger owned the restaurant, and it had been closed for a month—officially, this was the final day of its summer hiatus, during which it had been buffed, shined, and spruced up. Tomorrow it would open to the public again, but today it was ours. With the sun pouring in and reflected off its many mirrors, the room shimmered. A lone cellist played a Bach suite as we trickled inside.

Above the tables in Le Grand Véfour are small plaques in memoriam to those who occupied them. Mark and I sat side by side on Napoléon and Josephine's banquette. Our lamb medallions were drizzled with basil sauce this time, and our wedding cake was topped with pulled sugar roses. The freesia and lilies that Madame Ruggieri and I had chosen for the tables were almost unnecessary, upstaged by the room itself.

"I'm your wife," I whispered to Mark at some point during dinner. He reached around me on the banquette, grasped my hip and pulled me toward him, sensing my incredulity at the pronouncement. I wasn't thinking about how long, or if, we'd last. I simply needed to name what I had become, as if saying the word meant I had simultaneously transformed into a more true and worthy soul. But I didn't feel the least bit changed. Instead, I sensed I had boarded the finest and sturdiest of ships but was terrified of water and furthermore, it was too late for me to disembark. Now, my destiny was choosing me.

"I guess that makes me your husband," he whispered.

"Forever," I said, and shrugged, punctuating the word with finality, rather than doubt.

"That's the plan," he said. And as we toasted each other, he added, "you'll see."

The dining room was brightly illuminated, but white curtains covered the lower half of the windows, blocking the view. My husband, my family, my friends—we were safely contained in an island in the middle of Paris. All that was visible from my table was the sky, the green tops of the linden trees, and the limestone columns that have framed the gardens for over two centuries.

A few weeks later, I was back in Paris after our honeymoon, sorting through gifts of crystal and china, and I read in the paper about Guy Martin, the thirty-three-year-old chef who had taken over at Le Grand Véfour. Such things made headlines in France.

Two decades later, while planning the trip to Paris to commemorate our anniversary, I remembered that news story and was stunned to learn that not only was Martin still there, but in 2010, he'd bought the restaurant outright. Whether it was fate or choice or some kind of compromise that had carried him to this point, Guy Martin—like Mark and I—had remained devoted to the decision he made all those years ago. I was intrigued. I wanted to meet him and hear what he might have to say on the subject.

As I left for Paris, I was uncertain what awaited me. I suppose I wanted to recall the promise of my wedding day, to experience anew the splendid room, and to peer back on my less-weary self with eyes that were now two decades older, and two decades more married. It was a sensation I sought, an assurance that longevity, whether in a restaurant or a relationship, does not have to equal decrepitude. I wondered whether my marriage had measured up to the place where it began, or vice-versa.

I hadn't expected to make it this far. Three years ago, my relationship and all my beliefs were shattered when I fell, briefly, for another man. Had the object of my obsession wished it, I would have walked across the ocean to Africa, where he lived, to start a new life with him. But he didn't, and my heart splintered in the aftermath. Agonized, I broke down, unable to move from my bed for weeks and then months, as I stared out the window and flooded my pillow with tears for another man.

I reached to Mark to rescue me, and incredibly, he did. My husband saw me as more deserving of pity—or at least compassion—than punishment, and forgave me for what was certainly a betrayal, but also, in his eyes, a most human transgression. In retrospect, I chock it up to midlife and hormones and the insane need to try and stop the mirthless passage of years. We were quite roughed up by the episode, but once I emerged on the other side—alive, first of all, and stronger—there were no more doubts that we would stay together. Forget about people changing, moving apart, growing in opposite directions. For Mark, to fail would have been to acknowledge a twenty-year mistake, and he couldn't brook such a waste of his time and judgment. Plus, we had never stopped loving each other.

But Mark and I would have to celebrate that victory—and our milestone—together, later, at home. He was stuck stateside with a pressing deadline and besides, we were broke again and couldn't justify two tickets to France. So I would be dining solo at Le Grand Véfour. It wasn't at all what I'd hoped, but I was curious nonetheless and even excited, for both that transcendent realm of the meal that awaited me and for the fact-finding mission with Guy Martin that would accompany it.

———✥———

The day before my reservation at Le Grand Véfour, I retraced the path I took on my wedding day. I visited the palatial *mairie* off the rue de Bretagne where, after the ceremony, the mayor of the 3rd arrondissement handed us our official *livre de famille*, with blank pages for up to eight kids. Had the playground across the street been there on our wedding day? If so, I never noticed. Before I had my children, now fourteen and seventeen, a sandbox and jungle gym were all but invisible to me. Now I stood near the playground trying to remember how Mark and I had traveled the meaningful distance from the mairie to Le Grand Véfour. Had a car taken us? How did my friends get there? I didn't recall being a jittery bride, but I was surprised to have erased that detail as well.

This time, I took the métro to Bourse and walked over to the gardens, where I lingered over an al-fresco breakfast of café crème and a brioche. It was an April day erupting with color and heat, and I tried to imagine how the courtyard must have appeared long ago at this time of year, from up above in Colette's salon. "The Palais-Royal stirs at once under the influence of humidity, of light filtered through soft clouds, of warmth," she wrote. "The green mist hanging over the elms is no longer a mist, it is tomorrow's foliage."

After my coffee and stroll, I took the long ride back to my old neighborhood near Père Lachaise, where I was staying in a hotel. At the front desk I felt the ions shift in a blast of sensory memory; to my disbelief, standing beside me was one of my husband's dear friends, who had been a witness at our wedding. We were utterly stunned into silence and then, laughter. An Australian artist, he was living in Arles and had done the paintings in the hotel. I hadn't seen him in eight years, and his wife had recently passed away. Mark and I weren't able to attend her funeral service, and I still felt awful about it. We hugged, caught up on all our children, had a drink, and wondered where the time went.

The following day, upstairs at Le Grand Véfour, I met Guy Martin and explained the strange coincidence to him—and how pleased I was that my friend would be joining me for lunch. He wasn't surprised.

"This is a magical place in a magical setting," Martin told me. "There's nowhere else in the world like it. When you do an important celebration here—no matter what happens down the line—it will always lead to exceptional things."

When I walked into the restaurant, it enveloped me in the familiar. Twenty years seemed utterly insignificant—both the vestibule and dining room appeared untouched by the passing decades. But incredibly, nothing felt stale or neglected. It was there still, that gleaming lightness that made me feel like I was swimming in soda, and that heady sensation of being instantly transformed into someone of consequence. As I stood on the carpet in a pool of sunlight, I nearly ached with life. The room was still shiny and alive and bursting with sensual promise.

Although at first it seemed unchanged, upon closer inspection I noticed subtle nods to the present day—hidden fixtures brightened the female forms painted on the wall, and the lace curtains that once ran along the perimeter had been replaced by etched glass.

But the soul of Le Grand Véfour was still there, preserved not only in the décor but also in the traditional recipes, which Martin was constantly reinterpreting and updating. The point, he said, was to allow for the inevitability of change, and to let history propel you forward rather than weigh you down. Nothing stays the same, he insisted, because nothing ever can.

"I'm growing every day," he said. "The same goes for my cooking. It's not a static thing. It is always in perpetual motion."

I wondered out loud whether there was some wisdom to be gleaned here, and what I could extrapolate about life and marriage. Mark and I had survived, but I still sometimes wondered how I could wake up to the same person, every day, for the rest of my days here on earth. Martin said that in his case, the key was to remember the person he was back then, and to trust the impressions that had brought him there in the first place.

"When I came here from Savoie, the Palais Royal gardens smelled like home. I couldn't believe I was in Paris," he said. "The first time I pushed in the door of the restaurant, I gasped. It was just like that." He snapped his fingers. "It was a *coup de coeur*, like when you meet someone—you aren't certain, but you know something happened. You just know. I knew I belonged here."

In other words, I needed to envision the young man I'd fallen in love with, and trust that I would feel the same way about him if I met him today. I needed always to remind myself why it was Mark I'd chosen to marry. And I needed to recall the much younger woman I had been—the one who was never going to settle—and believe that even if I was guided somewhat by passion, I also possessed a good dose of sense to harness the free will required for a sound decision.

I closed my eyes and saw Mark and me with our limbs entwined, never imagining that I could one day be middle aged and scarred by an episode of doubt, looking to a Paris restaurateur to shine a light on my future while illuminating my past.

For twenty years, Martin had setbacks and dark times, and when Michelin took away his third star, it was his own version of weathering the infidelity that nearly destroyed my marriage—and certainly my faith in the institution. But as guardian of Le Grand Véfour's culinary legacy, he also led it into the twenty-first century with the same devotion that motivates those too optimistic, or hopeful, to entertain the idea of failure: hard work, flexibility, creativity, love.

"I never thought I'd be here for twenty years," he says.

"Tell me about it," I said.

"Sometimes I'm still surprised."

"Yes, me too," I said.

"But as long as I feel good here, and as long as I have faith in what I do, I'll stay," he said. "Life is very short."

That, I realized, could also mean, why bother? Other adventures and other paths constantly tempt every man and woman in this life, forever posing the question of whether it takes more courage to stay put or move on. After all, in marriage—and in food—twenty years is already no small achievement.

This time I sat in Jean Cocteau's chair with my old friend, who was here with us twenty years ago. It was a strange thrill to now feel my own history in this room. The chilled bottle of pink Champagne we drank was the same Mark and I had served at our wedding, probably the same kind I'd shared with Nicolas, and the same I'll drink with my husband on our fortieth anniversary. Even the food managed to be revelatory: Martin's modern turn on the Grand Véfour's classic ravioli, now prepared with the finest foie gras in the land, seemed to prove that the best use of the past is to chart the course for the path ahead.

Still, I missed Mark. He had alluded to his tenacity all those years ago, and because of it, I had something to celebrate. We had survived what for many couples would have been insurmountable. And if I could learn anything from a restaurant that had withstood centuries and wars and misfortune, and a chef who taught me that fidelity does not have to mean compromise, then we too would last forever.

I knew that just outside in the gardens, lovers kissed, babies tumbled, and a work crew trimmed the lawn, leaving the smell of cut grass. We could see none of it above the newly etched windows, just the sky over Paris—eternal, faithful, delicious.

Mouffetard: Of Markets and Meandering

Georgia I. Hesse

IN LATE MORNING WE WOULD meet at the tomatoes. We idled near the radishes and loitered among the lettuces: lettuces curly and lettuces flat; lettuces reticent and lettuces bold; lettuces by any other name than *Lactuca sativa*. We ogled withered back olives, those tiny, briny explosives.

We resisted fiddling our fingers among the fat, crimson cherries; did not manhandle the melons, their webbed nettings the shades of cheap jade, hiding orange flesh as fragrant as Provençal afternoons. We tweaked no plump peach cheeks nor did we snap the anorexic green beans.

We behaved rather well, I thought, in the sensuous street market at Place Mouffetard. We were, after all, shopping for a simple dinner. (Allen Ginsberg creaked in my ear near the carroty carrots: "Wives in the avocados, babies in the tomatoes!—and you, Garcia Lorca, what were you doing down by the watermelons?")

Though worthy of the strokes of a Gallic Georgia O'Keeffe, these are homely, humble plants, far removed from the insolent perfection of their California cousins. They are approachable. "Please take me home now," they beseech, "for I beg to be consumed in the very moment of my goodness."

Place Mouffetard announces itself with a pretty fountain near a clutch of sidewalk cafés and a *boulangerie* where baked irresistibles bask: crusty *baguettes* as long and stiff as swords, *bâtard* and *ficelle* and *boules* and *miches*, not to mention a portly *pain de ménage*. A nearby wine shop dedicates itself to the best of Bacchus while a small *supermarché* (today in France every *marché* is *super*) supplies Beaujolais, Muscadet, and other agreeably modest bottlings.

Rue Mouffetard (for me) begins here at the market square and it sashays north for a few corners to the leafy, fountain-centered Place de la Contrescarpe. It is the most rural, most village-like street I know in Paris, all friendly, familial bustlings and to-ings and fro-ings.

Another fountain, the Pot-de-Fer where Mouffetard meets the street of that name, spills surplus water from an aqueduct built by Marie de Medici to carry water to her palace, not far away in the Luxembourg Gardens.

The *Mouffe*, as the house-lined medieval lane is known to its familiars, served in the 13th century as the main street of a small market town overlooking the river Bièvre and supposedly derives its name (I know not how) from a district known as

Mont Cétarius. Angled across from the market, the church of St. Médard (1655) remembers a sixth-century counselor to the Mérovingian kings who had the happy habit of bestowing wreaths of roses upon virtuous maidens. (Are there others?) In the early 18th century, this church stared through its windows at throngs of hysterics tramping through its cemetery in search of miraculous cures. Louis XV was moved to nail a sign to the gate: "By order of the King, let God/ No miracle perform in this place!"

In anticipation of the revolution of 1789, the quarter swarmed with the wretched and the ragged, seditionists and mutineers whose only solace in a sorry life was a bottle of sour wine.

John Russell, chief art critic of the *New York Times* from 1982 to 1990 (he died in 2008) once described the "unpredictable Everyday" of Mouffetard: "I doubt if there is any other street in the world in which an eight-ounce *croquette of foie gras* can be bought with one hand and a *cornet de frites* with the other; or in which your neighbor at the bar may be either the General Secretary of the Académie Française or a starving Tunisian. And the noise of the Rue Mouffetard! It combines the monotony of Fez, the unending repetition of near-oriental cries, with what can be found only in Paris: the chop-chop of tongues that cut like the guillotine. . . . Few streets are more expressive than this companionable inferno."

This would be a good place to live, I've always thought, and for a short one summer we did, my sister and I, right around the corner at 8, avenue des Gobelins.

Making ourselves at home in Paris meant cozying into a neighborhood, our own curious corner of the 5 arrondissement. On our first morning, we tramped the territory, discovering "our" coffee bean and tea leaf shop, a *confiserie* (*chocolat* to live for), laundry and cleaners, bank and ATM, a Prisunic (for household odds and ends), more cafés than you could shake a *steack* at, a nearby métro stop (Gobelins), and one congenial *brasserie*, Marty, where the calendar is stuck in the 1930s and reporters from Le Monde come to carp and consume crustaceans.

But even in Paris, comestibles alone do not a city make.

In my own version of Paris' moveable feast, museums rest at the art of the matter. My menu begins with *hors d'oeuvres*— the Arts Décoratifs, the Mémorial de la Déportation, the Cognacq-Jay—continues with the *entrées* of the Musée d'Orsay, the Richelieu wing of the Louvre, the Cluny (National Museum of the Middle Ages), Musée de la Musique, the Carnavalet (Museum of the City of Paris), and concludes with desserts: the house of Victor Hugo in the harmonious Place des Vosges, the Musée Rodin, and the Musée Maillol.

This is the way we dallied through our days. Breakfast was prepared from fruits and breads bought the night before at Place Mouffetard, a saving of time and a greater one of money. Sometimes we métro'd to a museum first and collapsed later into a comfortable brasserie. Dusk brought a return to Mouffetard for dinner, occasionally at an unpretentious place near our 'hood: Au Moulin à Vent, mayhap, where little has changed since 1946.

Here, in Ralph Waldo Emerson's felicitous phrase, is how we "invited our souls."

Arts Décoratifs: Years ago, when I stepped reluctantly inside this treasury of taste and design, my enthusiasm for the *beaux-arts* did not extend to furniture, "soft" furnishings, wallpapers, textiles, or other interior embellishments. But that was before I had inspected Mme. de Pompadour's dainty desk (so-o-o unsuited to the computer age), revelatory of the 18th century's passion for oriental *objets*; before I had entered the Hoentschel Room, an extravagance (but not an excess) of Art Nouveau from 1900; before I had restrained myself from playing with antique toys.

In 1867, artists and businessmen began working in tandem to promote a revival of "beauty in usefulness." They succeeded. Spanning the centuries from the Middle Ages until today, the collections are displayed by theme (carpentry, faïence, enamel work, etc.) so that one can compare techniques as well as tastes by period.

Café Ruc is well-bred but unpretentious, with a carefully spiffed interior and bustling service at the sidewalk tables a few yards from Arts Décoratifs. If you need a *croque Madame* or an endive salad with Roquefort and walnuts, this is the place, across the traffic from one of my favorite, so-Paris inns, the Hôtel du Louvre (now a Hyatt), and the Comédie Française; (159, rue Saint-Honoré).

Mémorial des Martyrs de la Déportation: No one I have introduced to this severe crypt at the upstream tip of the Ile de la Cité has emerged dry-eyed or been inclined to speak.

Strangely, several friends have been unable to find this spot, just "behind" the great bulk of Notre-Dame and across the Quai de l'Archevêché. A few stone steps descend toward a fierce, wrought-iron grille beyond and below which flows the Seine.

The quiet crypt (a cave, a tomb) remembers some 200,000 French Jews and sympathizers whose lives were snuffed out in the hot summer of 1942, fuel for Hitler's Nazi fires. Small chambers to the left and right of a central marker replicate prison cells in which the deported—men, women, and eventually children—could be held until they faced the Final Solution. Blood-red inscriptions on the walls scream silently.

Within a long, dark tunnel extending from the grave of the Unknown Deported, each lost life is represented by a tiny light. Rows of them, uncountable to the eye, stretch back, back, into infinite gloom. It is impossible to contemplate the departure of 200,000 souls.

A message around the grave reads, "They went to the end of the earth and they have not returned."

Le Procope: The oldest café in Paris debuted in 1686, deriving its name from that of its Sicilian patron Francesco Procopio. It was lavish in decoratio—all mirrors, chandeliers, and gilt—and, restored, remains so. Here, the new drink from the Near East, *Kahve,* stimulated the brain, it was believed. Literary lights (Voltaire), political gurus (Benjamin Franklin), as well as starving artists and the smart set thronged its gorgeous rooms and still do, in its present incarnation as a temple of classic temptations and worldly flash; (13, rue Ancienne Comédie).

Musée Cognacq-Jay: His name was Ernest (Cognacq) and hers was Marie-Louise (Jay) and together they opened in 1869 what became the largest department store in all Paris, the Samaritaine. She had been the senior clothing saleswoman at Le Bon Marché, he was an admirer of the arts of the Enlightenment, and their store's name had a lucky ring to it, named for a water pump near the Pont Neuf (New Bridge, but the oldest in town), decorated with a figure of the woman of Samaria giving Jesus water at the well.

When the wealthy (and Good) Samaritaine owner died in 1928 (his wife had predeceased him), his private possessions became the property of Paris and today repose in the 16th-century Hôtel Donon in the Marais district. Twenty small, intimate rooms show off some well-known paintings (by Chardin, Watteau, Boucher, Tiepolo, Reynolds, etc., but in essence this is a home rather than a public museum. Porcelains, furniture, and carpets evidence a sense of comfortable, not showy, living.

Clearly, the occupants will return in a moment; (8, rue Elzévir).[1]

Ambassade d'Auvergne: Departing the 19th century and preferring not to be thrust too abruptly into the 21st, I like to settle into this cozily rustic world where roots of the cookery lie deep in the Massif Central. The *pot-au-feu* transports me to

---

1   La Samaritaine was acquired in 2001 by LVMH, the luxury group owned by France's wealthiest man, Bernard Arnault. The store was closed in 2005 for safety reasons and a redeveloped site was scheduled to open in 2016. However, work has stopped early in 2015 and is now the center of a civic row.

arrière-grand-mère's day, or would had she been French. The *auvergnat* cheeses and regional wines (Chanturgue, Châteaugay, Saint-Pourçain) insure my mellow mood; (22, rue du Grenier St-Lazare).

Musée d'Orsay: "The (railway) station is superb and has the air of a Beaux-Arts palace, and the Palace of Beaux-Arts resembles a station; I propose to Victor Laloux [the architect of the Orsay station] to make an exchange if there is yet time." Thus wrote the painter Jean-Baptiste Detaille in 1900, just before the inaugurations of the two structures.

Lo, only eighty-six years later, Detaille's vision came to pass, and in the 21st century the Orsay ranks among the most stunning museums anywhere, dedicated to works of art from the mid-19th to early 20th centuries. The Impressionist paintings lure the most Americans, but the exhibits are abundant and diverse: the tiny bust-sculptures of Honoré Daumier (delightfully evil or grumpy or sneaky-looking), a mock-up under plastic that allows "on top" of the Opéra quarter and a scale model of the Garnier Opera House seen from the inside, monumental sculptures, fanciful furniture that seems to have been trapped in a moment of dancing, and examples of early cinematography.

Restaurant du Musée d'Orsay: One would be silly to look elsewhere for luncheon when the museum houses this historic eatery, as magnificent as it was when it opened in 1900 in the former *Hôtel.* Superb furniture sets off the dazzling chandeliers and gilded ceilings. The whole is recognized as a Historic

Monument. Chef Yann Landureau presents traditional cuisine, interspersed with original dishes linked to the museum's shows.

Musée du Louvre: Few travelers need to be told about the *grandpère* of them all, born in 1793 as a *divertissement* for Everyman. Usually considered the largest single museum in the world, it shelters more than 300,000 of history's most valuable artworks. The inauguration of the Richelieu Wing in 1993 (to the disgust and dismay of the Ministry of Finance, which found itself evicted) and the Galerie Carrousel with its inverted pyramid and thirty-some shops kept the Grand Louvre Project awash in admiration and opprobrium until its completion in 1997. My favorite treasures in the Richelieu Wing come from Sargon II's Assyrian Palace at Khorsabad (2371-2316 B.C.). I remain awestricken by the remains of the medieval Louvre and its circular fortress-keep constructed for Philippe Auguste in the 12th century.

Grand Louvre is the traditional restaurant on the site; the trendiest, Café Marly; for self-service the Café du Louvre, La Caféteria; within the museum itself, Café Denon (restaurant, tearoom), Café Molien (summer terrace), and Café Richelieu (restaurant, tearoom, summer terrace).

Cluny: More than two thousand years ago, Romans conquered the city they called Lutetia (*Lutèce* in French) on the Ile de la Cité and the left bank of the Seine. (The Parisii, a Celtic people, had long inhabited the site, hence its once and future name.) Caesar's general Labenius set about structuring a Roman town incorporating a forum, three thermal baths, a theater, and an amphitheater.

Little of Gallo-Roman Lutetia remains: a hint of amphitheater, a *soupçon* of the arena (ambling distance from "our" house on the Avenue des Gobelins), some touching archeological finds (a child's Roman-style sandal) in the Musée Carnavalet (museum of the City of Paris) and vestiges of the baths. But those baths! Today, along with the reconstructed 13th-century residence of the abbots of Cluny, they house the absorbing collections of the National Museum of the Middle Ages. The vaulted *frigidarium* (for cold-water baths) still stands almost 50 feet high.

Balzar: Just a *saucisson's* throw from Cluny awaits this classic brasserie of the 1930s, with high ceilings, exquisitely dark woodwork, and mammoth mirrors that since 1979 have been hung at a discreet angle by the owner in order that he might observe untoward behavior. Although service in Paris in this century is unremittingly smiley and politically correct, I am somehow reminded at Balzar of the cranky (but compelling) old days when a regular customer who complained about a sauce might be snapped at by the *patronne:* "A-HAH! You've been ruining your taste buds at another restaurant!!" (6, place Paul-Painlevé.)

Musée de la Musique: Some twenty centuries following the building of the baths, this extraordinary museum opened its doors in January, 1997, in the relentlessly contemporary Parc de la Villette at the northeast reach of the city. For more than a century, until 1974, slaughterhouses and a vast cattle market had flourished there, made obsolete by progress in refrigeration technology.

Now La Villette is home to sixteen entities, including the City of Science and Industry (largest such museum in Europe), and La Géode, an IMAX theater inside a vast geodesic dome that used to house the world's largest screen. The Philharmonie de Paris, a symphony hall with 2,400 seats for orchestral works, jazz, and other noteworthy diversions, opened in January, 2015.

A visit to the self-contained city within a city (perhaps traveling one way by métro and the other by boat via the Canal St-Martin) can easily consume an entire day.

It's *la musique* that lures me most. Music sacred and music hip-hop, jazz and opera and baroque: all forms play here in perfect harmony. Some eight hundred instruments are displayed. We all know the violin, of course, the lute and even the clavichord, but who is familiar with the *serinette* (bird-organ), the *vielle à roue (hurdy-gurdy,* not barrel organ) or the *serpent militaire* (a kind of clarinet in the shape of a snake)?

Hearing is believing. Wearing earphones, we were astonished that instruments struck up at our approach; entire orchestras soared into sound as we stood before models of the château of Versailles or the imperial salon of the duke of Gonzaga at Mantua. Happily, the music does not bleed from one exhibition into the next and plays as long as one stands in place. Music thus joins architecture joins technology to present a symphony of artistic forms.

Café de la Musique in a separate building off the fountain-centered *place* offers a pleasant outdoor terrace in summer. Followers of the salons of yesteryear, however, might take the long walk or the métro to *La Chaumière,* an oasis of handsomely-laid tables, red velour armchairs and sparkling lamps that speaks of comfortable refinement. The cuisine is original and finely achieved with fresh products; excellent wine list; (46, avenue Secrétan).

Carnavalet: The vast museum that illustrates the story of Paris from prehistory to the present is at home in the only surviving 16th-century pile in Paris, the Hôtel Carnavalet, and the 17th-century mansion that elbows it, Hôtel Le Peletier-St-Fargeau, both in the trendy Marais district. In the former, the traveler with a literary bent pays respects to Marie de Rabutin-Chantal, a.k.a. Mme. de Sévigné, who in the 17th century sat within its stately salons to pen her windy, wonderful letters to her daughter, the erudite and overbearing Françoise-Marguerite, the Countess de Grignan. "Since one cannot have everything," Madame wrote on Oct. 7, 1677, planning her occupation of the Carnavalet, "we will have to forego parquet floors and the small new fireplaces now in vogue, but we will have a beautiful courtyard, a lovely garden and a fine neighborhood!" Indeed.

Today her digs present a room devoted to the famous beauty, but is more noted for its archeological remains from prehistory, the Bronze and Iron ages, Gallo-Roman Lutetia, the Mérovingian and Carolingian eras, up to the Bourbons and 1789, while Le Pelletier next door continues the tale from the Revolution to the present.

You don't know the Carnavalet? You can't know Paris.

Bofinger: In 1864 Frédéric Bofinger, an enterprising Alsatian, opened his eponymous restaurant (say not bow-finger but bow-fagn-JAY, please), if not Paris' first brasserie at least the first establishment to sell draft beer. This is the arche-typical brasserie in a setting that achieves ornate success while avoiding the florid: back lighted glass cupola with floral motifs, giant flower arrangements, carved wood, mirrored walls, bronze wall brackets, black leather benches, and decorative marquetry panels. Guests whisper over dessert about the restroom ceramics. Classic Alsatian dishes are the choice: *choucroute garni* (herbs, spices, smoked meats simmered in consommé and served with sauerkraut cured in wine and/or Champagne), *choucroute* with trout, fried carp, salmon, *foie gras*, chicken *vol-au-vent* (in cream sauce in a pastry shell), boiled potatoes, custard tartes studded with irresistible little Mirabelle plums. Not for nothing did Waverly Root characterize Alsace as the Domain of Fat. Yum; (5, rue de la Bastille).

Maison de Victor Hugo. The poet, novelist, and orator who ranks among the lions of French literature lived from 1832 to 1848 in a lovely townhouse in the handsomest square (I think) in town, the Place des Vosges. It's refreshingly small, provoc-ative, and strolling distance from the Carnavalet; (6, place des Vosges).

L'Ambroisie has created a cuisine that is ambrosia indeed, served in a regal setting with prices to suit. Bofinger could serve you well here, also; (9, place des Vosges).

Musée Rodin. From 1840 to 1917, the inspired sculptor Auguste Rodin lived in the splendidly rococo Hôtel de Biron, just across the boulevard from Hôtel des Invalides, which houses Napoléon's tomb. (Interestingly, Biron was selected by

Rodin's secretary at the time, the formidable German novelist Rainier Maria Rilke.)

The Rodin (since 1919) is small and the works are choice; it ranks among the most satisfactory museums in Paris. The ground floor serves as stage for such sculptures as The Cathedral, The Kiss, and The Walking Man. The first floor, reached by a magnificent 13th-century staircase, shows off smaller master-pieces and the familiar statues of Balzac and Victor Hugo. The garden is a joy, enlivened by the triumphs that made Rodin a cultural hero during his lifetime: The Thinker, The Burghers of Calais, and The Gates of Hell; (77, rue de Varenne).

Musée Maillol (a.k.a. *Fondation Dina-Vierny).* Opened in March of 1995, the beautiful old house devotes itself to the creations of Aristide Maillol in all their varied aspects: drawings, engravings, paintings, sculptures, decorative art, original plaster, and terracottas. That alone would make it worthwhile, but the museum also delights with the collec-tions of Dina Vierny, the artist's last model: masters of French naive art, drawings by Matisse, Degas, Picasso, Ingres, Cézanne, Suzanne Valadon; drawings and watercolors by Gauguin, sculptures by Rodin, paintings by Serge Poliakoff, and other works by Kandinsky, Marcel Duchamp, Jacques Villon, and little-known Russian artists.

A pleasant, small restaurant and a bookstore encourage idling; (59-61, rue de Grenelle).

Le Grand Colbert: For brasserie fare, go on to this townhouse that was home to Louis XIV's great bookkeeper, Jean-Baptiste Colbert, who purchased the home in 1665. Its latest transformation, in 1987, gave it the elegance it now possesses with molded glass panels, red velvet benches, copper bar, finely patterned mosaic floor, and a general air of easy opulence; (4, rue Vivienne).

Too soon it came time to leave our *domicile* away from home. As the car whisked us toward Charles de Gaulle airport and dawn gilded the slowly-flowing Seine, we sighed for the sights not seen—there are nearly one hundred museums in Paris—and the meals not eaten, the markets not explored.

Would we do it all again? Faster than you can pop a cork.

Poetics

Illusion is the first of all pleasures.

—Voltaire

Parfumerie

Anna Elkins

Men take musk from glands
of crocodiles and abdomens of deer
to blend with orange, cassia, lavender.

When perfumes were for hiding odor
they must have had a practiced strength—
animal oils disguising animal oils.

I wonder at the hygiene of my ancestors,
their fear of regular bathing,
their trust of small bottles.

I don't wear perfume—have
no heavy body smells to smother,
no days and days of unbathed skin

to mask in citrus. But if I wore a scent
I'd touch it to my blue-veined
wrists or thick-skinned joints—

exercising its essence. Someday,
I'll allow sweat and earth to accumulate
as they would, unrinsed, on my skin.

I will create my own oils of hours
and evenings. I will collect a history
of myself, until I begin to know the animal

itch of flesh. But tonight I shower, washing
away the fragrance of living, starting over
the moment I turn off the tap.

Paris Heatwave

Benjamin Sutherland

Late one sweltering afternoon,

I sunk my sweaty fingers

Into a sugary orange,

A sphere of lightning

That slickened and perfumed my hands.

Then I dug my thirsty mouth

Into this blaze of sweet pulp,

Like a god devouring a star.

Paris
Billy Collins

In the apartment someone gave me,
the bathroom looked out on a little garden
at the bottom of an air shaft
with a few barely sprouting trees,
ivy clinging to the white cinder blocks,
a blue metal table and a rusted chair
where, it would seem, no one had ever sat.

Every morning, a noisy bird
would flutter down between the buildings,
perch on a thin branch and yell at me
in French bird-talk

while I soaked in the tub
under the light from the pale translucent ceiling.

And while he carried on, I would lie there
in the warm soapy water
wondering what shirt I would put on that day,
what zinc-covered bar I would stand at
with my *Herald Tribune* and a cup of strong coffee.

After a lot of squawking, he would fly
back into the sky leaving only the sound
of a metal store-front being raised
or a scooter zipping by outside,
which was my signal
to stand up in the cloudy water
and reach for a towel,

time to start concentrating on which way
I would turn after I had locked the front door,
what shop signs I would see,
what bridges I would lean on
to watch the broad river undulating
like a long-playing record under the needle of my eye.

Time to stand dripping wet and wonder
about the hordes of people
I would pass in the street, mostly people
whose existence I did not believe in,

but a few whom I would glance at
and see my whole life
the way you see the ocean from the shore.

One morning after another,
I would fan myself dry with a towel
and wonder about what paintings
I would stand before that day,
looking forward to the usual—
the sumptuous reclining nudes,
the knife next to a wedge of cheese,
a landscape with pale blue mountains,
the heads and shoulders of gods
struggling with one another,
a foot crushing a snake—
but always hopeful for something new
like yesterday's white turkeys in a field
or the single stalk of asparagus on a plate
in a small gilded frame,

always ready, now that I am dressed,
to cheer the boats of the beautiful,
the boats of the strange,
as they float down the river of this momentous day.

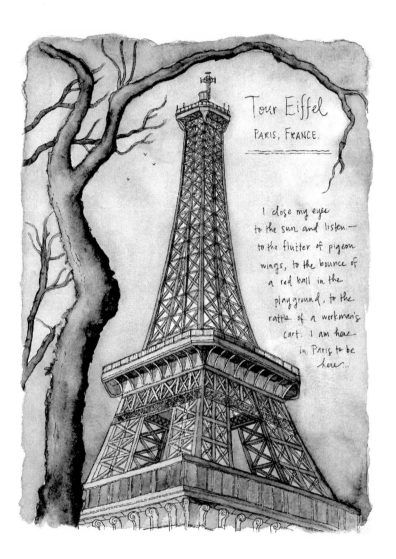

Tour Eiffel
PARIS, FRANCE.

I close my eyes
to the sun and listen —
to the flutter of pigeon
wings, to the bounce of
a red ball in the
playground, to the
rattle of a workman's
cart. I am here
in Paris to be
here...

Paris, je t'aime

He who contemplates the depths of Paris is seized with vertigo. Nothing is more fantastic. Nothing is more tragic. Nothing is more sublime.

—Victor Hugo

The Kiss

Kimberley Lovato

MILLE-NEUF-CENT-QUATRE-VINGT-DOUZE. 1992.

I'd practiced saying it over and over and it tongue-twisted my American mouth.

Across the Seine from the Eiffel Tower, the marble plaza of the Palais de Chaillot was slick from rain. A crowd of bundled revelers in knit caps and woolen scarves swayed and swigged Champagne, waiting to bid adieu to auld lang syne and herald in a new year.

A month earlier my roommate, Marie, had invited me to meet her in Paris for a week over the holidays. We would stay with her friend, not her boyfriend, she'd clarified, but a lover, a *je ne sais quoi,* she'd actually called him, Christophe. Paris was a place I'd dreamed of since first pinning a poster of the Eiffel Tower to my closet door in second grade, so I canceled my plans, drained my savings account for the plane ticket, and took off.

Christophe's third-floor walk-up apartment near the Porte de Clichy was dingy even in the daylight. My socks stuck to the pea green linoleum floors, and the bare bulbs dangling from the ceiling cast a garish halo on the flaking grey paint. There were no pictures on the walls; no curtains on the windows. From where I slept in the cramped living room, on a cracked brown vinyl sofa, I could watch the neighbors across the courtyard, their cigarettes burning bright orange then extinguishing in the dark. Parisian fireflies. Sometimes I'd hear Marie and Christophe making love in the bedroom. It was not the flowerbox appointed French *pied-a-terre* I'd watercolored in my mind. Outside, however, Paris blossomed.

In the mornings, Christophe took us to his favorite cafés where we warmed our hands around large fluted bowls of coffee, and gorged on croissants whose buttery confetti fluttered into my hair. We trailed him down into the métro stations, with their stale oily odor, and followed pink, blue, and yellow lines to stops whose names sounded like hamlets in fables: *Châtelet-Les Halles. Cluny-La Sorbonne. Strasbourg-St. Denis.* On sunny afternoons we massaged the gold lettering on the spines of antique books, and sometimes we'd huddle under our winter coats in the Luxembourg Garden, watching rose-cheeked couples hooked arm-in-arm crunch along the gravel paths. Come dusk, when shop windows twinkled with white fairy lights, we pressed our noses against the glass to ogle jewel-tone *macarons* and cherry-red Christmas packages looped with white satin ribbon.

At the end of the week, on the only table in Christophe's apartment, I opened a map and asked Christophe to point to where we'd been. His index finger retraced our routes, his hand briefly touching mine at the location of the Rodin Museum where we'd stood the day before, staring at the sculptor's sensual statue *The Kiss*. Heat rippled up my arm, along with a tinge of guilt that Marie's casual I-don't-know-what sent his French *oh-la-la* right through me.

Christophe owned two cassette tapes, one of which was Peter Gabriel's *Shaking the Tree* album and he played the first track, "Solsbury Hill," over and over. Sometimes he'd sing the lyrics as he shaved in the *petit-four*-sized bathroom mirror.

I giggled at his accent, but when he sang the line, "My heart going boom, boom, boom," mine thumped in unison.

Christophe's corner kitchen had a stout fridge, a minuscule oven, and a flimsy cabinet filled with a hodgepodge of glasses and one pot. Before heading out on New Year's Eve, Marie and I managed to roast a chicken and potatoes using a pan we'd fashioned from tin foil. We served our feast on mismatched plates and drank cheap red wine, which, I noticed, stained Christophe's two front overlapping teeth. After dinner he disappeared into the bedroom and came out wearing a cowboy hat atop his melt of chocolate curls.

"Howdy, " he said, a little drunk, raising a glass to toast to his *deux americaines*, calling us *adorables* and *charmantes*.

His eyes caressed my face until I had to look away.

The three of us arrived at the Palais de Chaillot a little after 11 p.m. but in the crowd's persistent push and pull, I separated from Marie and Christophe. A few minutes before the night's climax I found myself alone with thousands, counting down in front of Paris's famed landmark.

Three, two, one . . . Pop! Crack! Pshew!

"*Bonne Année!*" yelled strangers, who pecked both my cheeks. "Happy New Year!"

Fireworks splattered against the night sky, and burst inside me.

A hand touched my shoulder and spun me around. It was Christophe. He pulled me into his arms, my heart again going boom, boom, boom. His lips were wet and his eyes hunted for something in mine. And then he kissed me. I shouldn't have, but I let him. Slow and tender, deep and determined, his tongue rolling around my mouth like French candy.

The kiss lasted less than 10 seconds, and without saying a word, then, or ever, he squeezed my hands and walked away. I watched until his silhouette dissolved into Paris's resplendent mask.

I knew then I was in love.

The cliché and clandestine rendezvous at midnight with my roommate's *je ne sais quoi* was added kindling, but it was Paris that had lit the fire inside a young woman who'd stared at a poster all her life.

And I took something from Paris, too: a short-lived kiss along with the enduring desire stoked by *mille-neuf-cent-quatre-vingt-douze*, which has stayed with me every year since.

rules of etiquette for poets

Nicholas Adamski

it can't be about proving to everyone how smart you are
if you want to do that, go on a game show, like jeopardy

it can't be about proving that you don't care about life
if you don't care about life become a newscaster

it can't be about anything except writing it all down
everything you see and everything you feel

how you feel is so important and so true
your emotion is your connection to the earth and everything
on it

the more freely you share it the more blessings will rain down
upon you

lessons can be so difficult to hear the first time

heavens, I often have to learn a thing over and over to get it
straight
if the lesson comes from the inside of your being it can take a
lifetime to land

sometimes my mind is so thick i can barely see my hands,
sometimes
when all i want to do is this work, when all i want to do is
speak to you

whole years pass, inside, behind the windows and the doors,
in the beds
pacing the boards or simply wasting all of these gifts, I am
calling out

i can hear these calls, never faint, and i can go on sleeping
it doesn't matter that i know myself and that others call me by
my name

it doesn't matter at all that even the stars in the sky know
exactly who i am
all that matters has to happen here, in black and white

and on the planet, in the grass in the trees in the mud and the
vast ocean

we write our lives with our hands and our feet and we give it
away with our pens

and our hearts sing all the while without us even knowing
how is it possible that so much generosity functions within
our bodies

you could live in a forest for a life time
there is nothing to stop you

this planet is covered with food and shelter and joy
wings exist, there are animals that can breathe water

in my lifetime I have felt so much love
it is what my bones are made of

it is likely that your bones too are made of love and stones
how is it possible to go on living and miss so much

how is it possible to keep calling out for help
and keep receiving it
in my bed at night animals sleep beside me and beside each
other
somewhere, in factories and kitchens all over the world
people are making ice cream

i can hardly bear it, i know how absurd this is and i don't care
i am so in love that i can barely fit through the door

there are stones that speak to me, there are trees
and deer and whole mountain ranges know me by my name

i have more friends than i could ever count, they come to me
like waves
i will never tire of burying my feet in the sand

i will never tire of calling out your name
of telling you how much i love you

of how grateful i am for every single breath
and every time you walk through the door
and turn your head to look at me
once more

Mon Petit Bijou

Kimberley Cameron

"YOU HAVE BEEN FRENCH from the day you were born," my mother often told me as I grew up, as from an early age I loved all things French. Perhaps it started with my father taking me to the grocery store on Saturday mornings, for "our time," where I soon discovered miniature Princess Furniture. Why this was offered at a market still puzzles me, but they were collectables, definitely in the Louis XVI style, with gold trimmings, plush red velvet chairs, chandeliers and even a harpsichord, illustrated with a pastoral scene. My imagination was ignited by canopy beds and bookcases filled with old books.

Over many Saturday morning sojourns, I collected as much as I could, until I had the interior of a French château. It was my dollhouse and delight, and I still have the original boxes for most of the furniture.

I dreamt of living in elegance. We didn't have much money then, and the life I led was far different from the one I was able to envision. I played for hours, making up stories of myself as a princess sitting at the dressing table draped with sky-blue satin that even came with petite French perfume bottles.

I studied French as early as I could, and listened to Edith Piaf, and Henri Salvador. As a young woman, I drove around in my convertible listening to French pop, pretending that I was French. Even though I didn't understand the language that well, I watched every French movie I could. The work of François Truffaut influenced me greatly, and the writing of Emile Zola, and later Marcel Pagnol, immersed me in the world of Provence.

I frequented every French bistro I could find in America. Cheese soufflé and quiche sustained me. Although I lived in California, Chablis, Pouilly Fuissé, and red Burgundies were the wines to which I was drawn. I later discovered the Bordeaux region and tasted Pommerol, Saint-Émilion, as well as the Right Bank wines such as Margaux, Saint-Estéphe, and Pauillac. And of course, the rosés . . .

Although I yearned to go there, my first opportunity didn't arrive until I was thirty. It was a wonderful short visit to Paris and I took away memories of the way the light filtered through the trees in the Luxembourg Gardens, the enchanting stalls of the *bouquinistes* along the Seine, the sidewalk cafés, and the magnificent museums that held treasures I had never imagined. Every street beckoned with delightful surprises, and I often walked without a map, just finding my way instinctively.

I deeply felt that I had previously been in Paris, and recognized streets that I may have walked before, perhaps in another life. I felt I belonged there, and went back as often as I could, but staying only briefly. The emotional connection was fierce, especially when I gazed at the Eiffel Tower, the symbol of Paris. I wanted to be a part of it, and always dreamed I would live there someday.

As a young adult, my son had the opportunity to study for six months abroad, and when he was accepted to the American University in Paris, I knew it was fate for me to be there at the same time. It was the occasion of my fiftieth birthday, and I decided to see if we could find a rental for two months. The only stipulation was that it had to have a view of the Eiffel Tower. My husband thought I was *folle* (crazy), and would never find one, but I finally found an *appartement* looking directly at it.

That first night when the lights lit up the tower, I was riveted to the same spot for three hours, watching and waiting as the magic happened. Every hour, as soon as it started to twinkle, a collective gasp was heard as Paris sparkled.

A few days into the journey, as I waited for my husband in the foyer of the apartment, I told the concierge, "*Il est mon rêve d'avoir un appartement à Paris.*" It is my dream to have an apartment in Paris. She asked if I would like to see one. I stammered, "In this building?" "*Oui,*" she said, "*maintenant?*" Now.

The apartment needed lots of work, but it did have one window that looked onto the Champs des Mars, and La Tour Eiffel.

We had recently been introduced to a young architect/designer by the name of Jean-Louis Deniot, who I asked to take a look, just to see if we should buy it; I did not imagine that he would even consider a job this small—it was just under 1,000 square feet, and he was remodeling palaces in India.

Jean-Louis was like a cat, more like a panther, studying every wall and corner, and finally pronounced "If you buy this apartment—*je le ferai!*" He would do it.

When we were deciding what kind of look I wanted the place to have, he opened a book of table legs—yes, that's right, table legs. I kept pointing to the same ones and he declared, "Louis XVI!" One year and a half later we had our *petit bijoux,* little jewel box. When the tower lit up, I was transfixed, watching everyone pose for photos in front of it. *Tout le monde* seemed so happy to bask in its iron presence.

A few years later, the apartment was featured in Architectural Digest. The title of the article was "*À la mode*; Designer Jean-Louis Deniot Conjures a *Couture*-Quality Paris Flat that Makes an American Client's Dream Come True."

The ghosts of the princess furniture that I played with had became my real life. We spent many years there, enjoying the charm that Paris offers. My French improved, and soon the *vendeurs* at the open *marchés* came to recognize me, for we hosted dinner parties with countless *verres de Champagne* in our salon.

I eventually realized that Paris also carries with it the problems that come with large cities, and decided to say *au revoir.* The more mature me is now spending a little more time in the South of France, and the same girl loves it there, too.

I realize now that this place that so long ago I yearned to travel a great distance to reach, is a state of mind. I can return to Paris anytime I wish; I carry it in my soul.

Perspectives

It is the function of art to renew our perception. What we are familiar with we cease to see.
The writer shakes up the familiar scene, and as if by magic, we see a new meaning in it.

—Anaïs Nin

Pas de Deux in Paris

Jayme Moye

I FELL OUT OF LOVE WITH PARIS within hours of my arrival in 2007, my virgin time overseas. The city I'd long admired from afar I found to be harsh and chaotic up close.

Maybe it's because I was a *touriste*—another gawker shuffling through the city's overrun sites, from Notre-Dame to the Arc de Triomphe to the Louvre. What I remember most about that trip are the throngs of people: navigating jam-packed city sidewalks, cramming into the subway, waiting in an endless line to go up the Tour Eiffel. By nightfall, I'd be exhausted—an introvert done-in by the constant crowd. "Can we just get pizza and go to bed?" I'd plead.

Back then, I was feeling like a fish out of water in other aspects of my life too. I was married to my hometown sweetheart, in what was becoming a stifling relationship. And I was working as a database analyst for a technology firm, in what increasingly felt like a mismatched career choice. In retrospect, I was living a lie, following someone else's roadmap for happiness—go to college, get married, earn six figures, buy an expensive house.

Eight years later, I return to Paris a butterfly, a *papillon*, having broken free from my inauthentic chrysalis. A few years ago, I sold the house, ended the job, and left the marriage. I've since been trying to better align my life with my values: building a wealth of experiences, not possessions, and working for something more than the money—as a travel writer.

I hope this trip will be different, too. As the plane touches down, I'm buoyed by the fact that I have something to offer Paris other than just my tourism dollars. I'm here to promote a book that contains one of my stories, *The Best Women's Travel Writing, Volume 10*.

But as I walk to baggage claim in the Charles de Gaulle Airport, I'm immediately confronted with the harshness I recall from the first trip. An unsmiling Frenchman with darkish hair and darkish clothes marches doggedly toward me. If I don't step aside, he'll walk straight into me. I vow to hold my ground, and clear my throat to indicate my position. He doesn't raise his eyes, let alone adjust his trajectory. I brace for impact. At the last possible moment, he turns his shoulders and hips, just enough to reduce the head-on-collision into an uncomfortable brush-by. I realize I'm holding my breath.

Paris and I are off to an awkward start.

That evening, I meet up with three other women writers, Erin, Candace, and Anne, also Americans, at a flat on Île Saint-

Louis. Like me, they have stories in the anthology and we'll be reading together. I'm excited, but guarded—this is Paris after all. Champagne is poured as the setting sun softens the light outside the floor-to-ceiling windows. We sit and sip; going over the four scheduled talks we have planned for the week. Tonight I'll be up late, which will be a Paris first. Our event doesn't even start until 21:00. I wonder aloud if I'll be up for it. "You will," says Erin, who visits often. "Paris is different at night." I want to believe her.

We finish the Champagne and cheese and head outside to hail a cab. "*Au Chat Noir, s'il vous plaît*," says Anne, who does the best French accent of our group. We weave through the bar to the staircase in the back. Downstairs, a stone grotto marks a small stage, set behind benches four rows deep to create an intimate theater. David, a man dressed in jeans and a jaunty top hat welcomes us to "The SpokenWord Paris," where presenters get five minutes to take the stage and charm a multinational audience, who is just beginning to gather.

It's a venue well-suited to writers and poets, as well as budding comedians and performance artists. I'm scheduled to read an excerpt from my story about a trip to Afghanistan, right after a Romanian woman sings a Fiona Apple song in her second language. We find seats and, over the din of French and English and what I'm pretty sure is Portuguese, place an order for four glasses of wine. Erin might be right about Paris at night. This is my kind of place.

Afterward, adrenalized by the stage and emboldened by the wine, I venture out into the cool evening air with my boyfriend, a French-Canadian, who in our two years together has proven to be an excellent match. We don't have to look far to find a place to eat and drink—the street is alive with brasseries, bistros, bars, and cafés. We duck into Café Justine, drawn by the rich, dark wood paneling and large windows. Inside, couples and small groups of friends sit close together, deeply engrossed in their wine and conversation.

We order a bottle of Côtes du Rhône, a *roquette* salad, and *boeuf bourguignon*, accompanied by crusty bread. The night is no longer young, but the waiter doesn't seem to mind. It's as if time has lost its value, having been replaced by more important concerns like the swirl of red wine in a glass, the smile of a loved one, the last bite of dessert. By the time we step back out into the street, it's after 2:00 a.m. and we're a long way from our flat. "Let's walk," I plead. I don't want this night to end.

The next morning, I sleep until noon. We're staying in a blissfully non-touristy section of Montparnasse, complete with one of the best markets in the city. Since I don't have to be anywhere until the next event that evening, and because there are no throngs of people on these streets, I decide to explore.

After rustling up some quiche and black tea at the market, I come upon an old stone wall I'd noticed at the end of the street. It turns out to be a cemetery, although upon stepping through the entrance gate, it feels more like a museum. In addition to headstones are sculptures, monuments, statues, and even works of art. Thousands of trees share the space. It's hauntingly beautiful, and serene, and completely unexpected in the big city. As I meander through the tombs, I realize I could spend hours here—which I just so happen to have. I see only a handful of others that afternoon, in what I later learn is Cimetière Montparnasse, the final resting place of many of Paris's famous artists, writers, and intellectuals.

"Where were you the first time I was here?" I ask the angel statue in the center of the cemetery's grassy roundabout. I imagine his divinely arrant reply: "Where were *you*?"

That evening, I ride the métro to Shakespeare and Company. I exit at Saint-Michel and climb the stairs, emerging from beneath the streets into the moonlight. I'm standing at a particularly large intersection and take a moment to orient myself, looking for Rue de la Huchette, the road that leads to the bookstore. I get the sensation I've been here before.

Sure enough, walking down rue de la Huchette, I experience a déjà vu: the "I Love Paris" t-shirt stands, the black menu boards with handwritten restaurant specials blocking the sidewalk, the vertical spits displaying meat for gyros behind glass windows, a cacophony of dance music and jazz pouring out onto the street. This is where my flat was located on my first visit to Paris.

Near the end of the street, I pause beneath the third-story window of my previous flat. I remember its parquet floor and elegant Neo-Classical décor. But most of all, I remember journaling about my disappointing trip, seated in a high-backed chair at the mahogany desk on the other side of that window, keeping the curtains drawn.

It dawns on me that back then, I wasn't aware that one of Europe's most famous bookstores was just around the corner.

That one day I'd be presenting there, reading my own writing from a book. I tilt my head back and close my eyes, smiling, basking in the light of the Paris moon. I'm so close, yet so far, from the place I was eight years ago.

A group of animated university students brings me back from my reverie. I'm still smiling as I continue across the street—until I notice a smartly dressed man walking straight toward me. Not this again. I steel myself to maintain position. But something has changed inside. I no longer feel so unyielding. Instead, I feel curious. I walk confidently toward the man, and at the last possible moment, I shift my own hips and shoulders. *Voilà*—the Parisian and I slide by each other in perfect synchronicity. I exhale.

Yes, Paris is different at night. This time, I'm part of the dance.

Abstract Photograph

David Leo Sirois

I walk along rue de la Convention
9 o'clock at night
on a Thursday   this 18th day of April   2013
I may never comprehend this
silver-colored abstract photograph
its long uncomplicated electrified rail
1900 anno domini silver dollar moon's blank stare   follows
citizens of the city
Time is tracking me down whether I sit stand or walk
Hold the beat that moves the unsaid drum
to count myself out
to act & not to act
How to unwrap the real
Timeless tireless invisible music
enters the senses without resistance

The inevitable leaf
Yellow gold red astronomical clocks the size of my own hand
How do I learn how to surrender
Rigid branch & brittle leaf
bristling fingers rattling air
speak to my sentient spine
Wide wide libraries of things I don't understand
What time is this that makes me question
motions of our measurer
who celebrates perpetual remembrance
I come unhinged   gripping raw seconds
enter the underworld   roots of the wild violet
You the river that rolls through the eye of a needle
You the stone partition that keeps me from the water
You are seven-story dwellings that keep us trapped
in boxes eating sandwiches
The sound of profound pounding drums in August heat
Back of my neck pulsing
Resounding windchimes fill voids inside night
The sound arises in ice-encrusted snow underfoot
Green buds hover where golden rain had filled the forsythia
How should I proceed in this web of wrought-iron railings?
The sound arises with Appalachian mountain dulcimer
whispers
shapes so many moods the endless turning time alone
The sound devises methods of piercing the heart
The sound alive and interested in finding what I seek
I see the sound at twilight

Walk delicately along the edge of this bridge

How small I am the toothpick bones

How wide the opened souls

How my whole head is in flames unseen

A silver shiver shakes my spine

Silence waits for its chosen time

A Very Long Engagement

Catherine Karnow

PARIS HAS BEEN IN MY LIFE for as long as I can remember. My father lived there in the fifties, as a student on the G.I. Bill, then worked his way up to become a journalist at Time-Life. He and my mother, both Brooklyn-born, met in Algiers and their romance flowered in North Africa and in Paris, where my mother modeled for Chanel and Dior. They got married in Gibraltar and moved to Hong Kong, where I was born and grew up.

Throughout my life, my parents sprinkled their conversation with French words and phrases. My mother often started her sentences with *en principe* or ended with an exclamatory *"C'est pas possible!"* By the time I was in college, I was fairly fluent. To know the language and culture of France was to be educated and sophisticated. It was my dream to live in Paris some day; I felt I would be right at home. But my relationship with Paris would not be easy to cultivate.

To encourage both my French education and my photography, my father arranged a *stage* for me at Magnum Photos when I was fifteen. I was studying photography in high school and the Magnum photographers defined my style, which was black-and-white, photo-journalistic street photography. Henri Cartier-Bresson, Marc Riboud, Bruce Davidson, Ian Berry, Eve Arnold—I treasured their images. That summer I lived with family friends and walked every day to rue Christine, in the chic part of Saint-Germain. The Magnum bureau had floor-to-ceiling shelves holding boxes of work prints, and it was my job to keep the boxes sorted and to refile the prints after photo-buyers looked through them.

In my free time I would look through binders of contact sheets, searching for a favorite photo to see exactly how the photographer got that shot. For example, Cartier-Bresson's famous photo of a family picnicking by the river took him four frames. In the first shot, the family is sitting, their backs to the camera, facing the water. In the next, there is a slight movement with one person. In the third frame the man with the black hat turns slightly to his right and pours a bottle of wine: the Decisive Moment. And in the fourth and final frame, he is staring angrily at Cartier-Bresson. One can imagine the entire scenario and understand Cartier-Bresson's method precisely. Magnum photographers shot all over the world, but I especially loved looking at their images of Paris. I found even the gritty photographs poetic.

After work, I would go out and shoot. I randomly chose a métro stop and then shot in that neighborhood until dark. The next day, Magnum sent out my black-and-white film to be developed, and made contact sheets or prints as I chose. At the end of my *stage* I had earned the equivalent of $20—I'd had no idea that the lab costs were coming out of my salary! I had been planning to travel for a couple weeks after the job ended, but I couldn't go anywhere on $20. My boss, seeing me in tears of shock and dismay, gave me an extra $50, which allowed me to travel to the photography festival in Arles. Marc Riboud at Magnum had assured me that the photographer Elliott Erwitt would "take care of me." Erwitt had no such interest. As I sat crying outside Erwitt's hotel, a Spanish guy approached me and we ended up camping on an island off Hyères.

The next summer, I found myself back in Paris after two impoverished weeks at the Montreux Jazz Festival, where a friend who had promised to lodge and take care of me never showed up. I stayed in Montreux until my money ran out, and then took a train to Paris, where I knew I could stay for free at Shakespeare and Company, the famous Left Bank bookstore. If the owner George Whitman found you to be intellectual and educated, he would let you stay upstairs, in what was affection- ately called the Tumbleweed Hotel. He liked me because my father was a famous writer and my Harvard-educated brother had written a novel one summer upstairs at Shakespeare's.

I arrived at Shakespeare's with no money whatsoever. I slept in the front room with the view of Notre-Dame. My mistake was to sleep *in* the bed rather than on it, and I woke up covered in large red bedbug bites.

I went to weasel some money out of my father's banker, André, who took one look at me and asked his secretary to put me in a fancy hotel, where they were doing noisy construction right outside my window at dawn. Realizing that the hotel cost was coming out of my father's bank account, I moved back to Shakespeare's and slept in my sleeping bag. Nobody I knew had any money back then, of course, so we used to eat dinner at *Les Balkans* around the corner, where they had a nineteen-franc menu and the *plat* was some form of chicken or pork fat. Sometimes all I could afford was a gyro, or a thirteen-franc couscous. I was always hungry.

George Whitman was a gruff man who sat downstairs at the desk, smoking cigarettes and staring off into somewhere, occasionally growling about the French authorities coming round to pester him for tax payments, or the building's other tenants being bothersome. In the evenings, George was in the kitchen making fruit compote, sometimes putting it in the freezer to make ice cream.

Years later, I saw him in a dim lunch counter in New York eating blueberry pie. I looked at him curiously and he just nodded, the hint of a smile flickering across his face.

In college I took a semester off and lived in Paris with my boyfriend, Jimmy, and best friend, Brian, who were studying semiotics and film theory at the Sorbonne. We found a shabby apartment near the Gâre de l'Est, where the window in Brian's minuscule room looked out into our living room. Every morning, he would throw open the window and, pretending to inhale fresh air, exclaim, "What a beautiful day!" In the evenings, fellow students would come over, smoking cigarettes, drinking wine, and pontificating about film and feminist theory. I fled to Shakespeare and Company frequently, and read the whole of Lawrence Durrell's *Alexandria Quartet*.

In 1984 after graduating from college, I moved to Paris, and looked for work in photography. Month after month, I found nothing and finally gave up. But I stayed, borrowing money from my father. I slept on couches, stayed in random apartments and was generally miserable. My father encouraged me to hang in there, as he had in his early days in Paris. For a brief period I worked at a sandwich shop, which prided itself on having "American" sandwiches, with names like the "Bogart", the "Elvis" and the "Marilyn." The job paid very little, but I got a free sandwich each day. I didn't have any money for film, so I couldn't really take pictures. I spent my days just walking around looking into fancy shop windows, sometimes trying on clothes, pretending I could afford them.

The worst temptation was the *traiteur*, the fancy deli with its Gruyère tarts, salmon mousses and mini pizzas. Golden chickens roasting on a spit outside sent wafts of painfully delicious smells down the street. I remained always hungry, but to make matters worse, I somehow gained twenty pounds from all the bread and cheese I ate. I lasted nine months in Paris, and feeling dejected, returned home to live at my parents' house. Once again, I had not been able to make Paris my home.

Over the years I returned many times to Paris, for work as a photographer and on holiday. I often stayed with André, my father's friend. He took me to fancy restaurants and taught me true old-world etiquette, and how to behave correctly in civilized society. To this day, I never set my plate aside in a restaurant when I am finished eating; André taught me that it's an insult to the waiter.

André lived in an enormous apartment in the 16th arrondissement, the grand old bourgeois neighborhood of Paris. I would sleep in his parents' room, a masterpiece of art deco style, with sixteen-foot high ceilings and a four-poster bed with an old sagging mattress. The splendid bathroom had a curved green-tiled sink, bathtub and bidet, but the plumbing hadn't worked for decades. Whenever André and I stayed in for dinner, his long-time housekeeper, Sophie, would serve us at the formal dining room table, set with silver and crystal, a decanter for the wine, and starched white napkins. The formality of André's lifestyle unsettled me, though I was fond of him just the same.

My family considered André to be our French *papa*. He had no wife or children and in turn loved us as family. By chance I was in Paris when he was declining. On the phone, he had enthusiastically invited me to stay, but I was unaware that he had been in a state of delirium during that call. I had come to Paris on assignment for *National Geographic* and arrived at his apartment with my luggage and cases of camera gear. His brother and sister were horrified to see me, and to my great sadness, they would not let me see him. In their eyes, I was not family, and it was not correct. I never had the chance to say goodbye.

In my younger years in Paris, I never felt quite comfortable, despite my fluent French. Maybe it was me, maybe it was the Parisians, but I always felt like a scruffy American girl, even when I wore heels and the requisite scarf tied just right, as the French women do it. Paris feels different now that I am in my fifties. I love that the French actually find women "of a certain age" to be attractive. There isn't that sense of being invisible, as we can sometimes feel elsewhere.

Paris has changed. There is a new generation, impatient and frustrated with French bureaucracy and stuffy tradition, a generation eager to forge ahead with new ideas in cuisine, art, technology and business. There are cool neighborhoods with coffee bars, restaurants with communal tables and inventive food; waiters who greet you with a smile and think your American accent is adorable.

I have fallen in love with Paris, maybe for the first time. The French say that a real friendship takes years, and we have weathered so much in four decades. Maybe it is the bittersweet struggles of all those years that has made ours a true love story.

The Top-Hatted SpokenWord Poets of Paris

SpokenWord Paris is one pole of a nomadic tribe of people who love poetry, writing and song.
A home for creatives and lost anglophones.

—SpokenWord Paris website

Phantom of the Opéra Station

Alberto Rigettini

As soon as I arrived in Paris, I started looking for a fight club. You know, those places where people kick each other's asses in order to relax from urban stress. Once in a bar I noticed a man with a long white scar going down his nose. It cut from his lips all the way to his chin and I asked him about it.

"Look in the underground," he said.

I started hanging out in alternative music venues. Nothing. SpokenWord events. Rave parties. Illegal milongas. Back alleys. Squats. Sewers. Catacombs. Whorehouses. Pissotières. Gay saunas. Nothing. Until I realized the guy who told me to look in the underground meant the underground meaning the underground. "Le métro." *Bien sûr*. The secret meeting point is on line 1 from 8 a.m. to 9 a.m. from Charles de Gaulle Étoile to La Defense. And there is another fight club on line 3 from

St. Lazare to Republique. You start seeing aggressive looking people walking down the stairs ready for the fight, which starts as soon as the train arrives and opens its doors.

Grappling holds, pinning holds, pain compliance holds, extreme petting, sixty-nine pins, dry foreplay, all kind of penetrative dressed sex, chokeholds, chinlocks, Boston crab locks, the camelclutch, the clothesline, the Fujiwara armbar, the Half Nelson choke, the vertical scrape on the face (typically feminine) and the outrageous V fingers in the nostril. Not to mention that infamous native Samoan move: with two fingers, expanding the opponent's mouth until the other collapses from pain. It happened to me. Someone from behind took me like this. It's terrible. You faint and you wake up in desolate and forgotten stations like Asnières sur Seine, Malakoff, Rue de la Pompe or Campo Formio.

And that's just bare-handed techniques. But commuters never travel unarmed. They can pierce you with plastic forks because they keep eating little Carrefour plastic salads while standing—*Ah! Ah! Ah! These little forks are fuckin' sharp!*— or they can use their pens, briefcases, umbrellas, strangle you with their headphones strings. Of course they will not forget to say: "*Pardon Monsieur*" or "*Excusez-moi, Mademoiselle.*" But politeness is just the posh side of war and violence begets violence. I don't want to be a sissy about it but I saw people walking down the stairs with sticks and fighting dogs. You might say they are blind and indeed they are entitled to spread some blind violence, but for me that's going too far and we see the consequences. Recently several people have died down there. I'm sure you've heard about the serial killer of the métro. All the Parisian newspapers talked about it. The killer randomly pushed commuters standing on the platform down into the tracks, into the incoming train. All the victims were killed at the same hour, 7 p.m. in the same station, Opéra on line 3. Curiously enough, nobody saw anything. That's why they started calling the killer The Phantom of the Opéra Station.

As you may remember, according to the original story by Gaston Leroux, The Phantom of the Opéra hides in the thirteen stories of tunnels under the Opéra House that lead to a subterranean lake. The phantom is jealous of anyone who approaches the pretty chorister Christine and he gets violent. What is true is that there are tunnels under the Palais Garnier (like everywhere underground Paris) and the Opéra house is built over an artificial lake. Nowadays, we are invading his hide-out and the Phantom seems to be jealous of any man on the crowded platform who presses his body against a young blonde employee of an insurance company, reincarnation of Christine. Enchanting ghost story but I prefer the bare truth.

We, the commuters, are all serial killers. We all killed together. Let's admit it. Do you know how it is when you alight on the platform of Opéra station line 3 during rush hour? Marching closely together, like Roman legionaries in tortoise formation or like can-can dancers in a quadrille, we walk down the first flight of steps, we cross over, we climb up, we turn right, we turn right, we walk down the stairs again, we turn left, we turn right, we hear the train coming and we walk faster and we run down the stairs, we reach the platform and aaaaaaaaaaahhhhhhh sprack!!! Oops. "*Pardon.*" Some unfortunate poor being in the front row might have been pushed too far.

We are all Phantoms of the Opéra Station. All the commuters are phantoms and not only under at Opéra. All the commuters are phantoms not because they kill but because they are already dead. It's no coincidence they are underground. Hell's always been underground. Have you ever talked with a commuter about this very subject? Commuters think they are paying for what they did in a previous life or in a previous job, and at best they hope that in the next life they will be travelling on another line. They feel they are doomed in a numbered circle of hell. Apparently the numbers of the lines follow Dante's order.

Line or circle 1 is for the innocent pagans (mostly tourists), line 2 for carnal malefactors, perverts and sex offenders, line 3 for junkies, winos and gluttons, line 4 for the greedy, beggars and pickpockets, line 7 for the violents against themselves, the suicides, the profligates, sodomites and fashion victims; on line 8 the false prophets, flatterers and hypocrites and so on. This lack of hope for the future mixed with feelings of guilt towards their past is visible on their faces and postures. You probably got used to it and you think it's normal to see faces like these in the metro. But tell me the truth: If you saw these faces gathered in any other room in the world you'd run away instead of stepping in, wouldn't you? And yet, inexplicably when the sliding doors open, you step in. Step right up ladies and gentlemen, feast your eyes on:

The hipno-rabbit.

The rancorous underbite.

The man who cannot close his mouth.

The woman who never had an orgasm and blames you.

The creepy sad clown.

The sniffing weirdo.

The gazing fish.

The gill man.

They weren't like that, years ago. Their parents have no protruding teeth. No underbite. No bulging eyes. It's not genetics. It's adaptation. It's commutation. They are mutating in order to survive their environment. He needs that face to survive his nine stops. She thinks that's the best posture to manage the everyday hassle. One hour a day for a few years and that's it: He can't close his mouth anymore. His muscles are atrophied, his bone structure oxidized into that wince. Smiles take two years and are turned down forever. One year to become a straight line. Two years to bend it downward. It takes the strength of bending bullhorns, only you have it.

Now I have an idea for an exhibition. I want to be sponsored by the Paris City Council. I will take hundreds of selfies, me smiling, extremely happy, surrounded by all these long faces. These pincers jaws. These efficient wrinkles. These eyes, slanted, like stabs. I look him in the eye and this time I can't stand it anymore. I put my fingers on his face and I force him to open his eyes.

"What the fuck are you doing?!? My eyes are like that!"

"No, they're not. Admit it and release your eyes. Relax. Surrender. Let the light come in. Plop your bulbs into my palms. My hands will heal your wounds."

It was a tough thing to do, I know. I had guts 'cause what kind of psycho they think you are while trying to spread a guy's eyes?

But you know what? I give up. He won't follow my advice. He keeps his eyes half-shut. He doesn't want to see the same stuff every day. Halving his eyes, he thinks, he'll half the time. And it's true. Soon the images will be all the same, flashing into dark windows. Goldfish in a bowl, they will develop a seven-second memory in order to forget minutes, hours and so on, centuries and millennia, turning into primordial stromatolites, the train rattling into the deep like a crushed can.

Quatre Poèmes sur les Pigeons

David Leo Sirois

Pigeon Convention

After the state of automatic temperature regulation in select
European marketplaces conference
there happened a much-anticipated gathering   feathers
displaying welcome
Whole baguettes blessed sidewalks
Never again would birdsong be the same
in this métropolitain wonderland of man-made parks & wild
concrete
Porte de Versailles convention organizers   & catering corps
complained
that these birds could be so finicky   they refused fresh
Madeleines
The air was filled with continuous cooing

Beak-to-beak encounters   Small discussion clusters
The air was all a-chatter   & pavement a-patter
Nothing mattered more than fallen crumbs

Looking

This handsome pigeon   looking smart
in his silver-grey suit   frequents singles sites
embellishing his height   & the growing group of
books he   has   gigs he has played
& all the starry hands he has shaken
The description of his interestingness continues to lengthen
Like any other singer   he awaits that Big Break
almost patient   about cooing into some bird's ear
His personal profile is clear—
sensitive   creative   oh-so-humble gentleman with wings

Dear Mirror

Comes a time in a pigeonette's life
when even silver & gold
could be sold for my dear eau-de-toilette Self-Pity
It's like, trendier than broken bits of blueberry muffin
I'm tempted to stare into sorry mirrors of sidewalk pools
No grinning Narcissus but an Echo of one soulful hopeless note
You, You, You with a counterpoint of *What am I?*
To whom do I belong? When strangers stare   with utter disgust
I can absorb the poisoned sting   or continue to sing

Queen of Beggars

I watched a white & one-legged pigeon in Place Emile Zola
Her nails were immaculately done & she
was the object of children's attention
I accidentally dropped a shred of tomato
& a mayo-coated chicken chunk   instantly gone
A boy of maybe 3   with hair bright black
pointed saying "Blanc! Blanc!"
while seeking my stranger's eyes
& drifting near   as his childminder
firmly grabbed him by the mind
It was then this bird extended
her hidden leg   which lacked 2 talons

Travel by Train
David Barnes

THE THUNDER OF THE TRAIN passing through the cutting makes the bridge shake. Its narrow arches, its great weight, these measure the train. The silence when it has receded is emptier than before.

I was ten when the hot air balloon skimmed the railway embankment, the pilot using the final roars of the gas burner to coax it over and dock with the ground. The orange bulk of the balloon staggered to a stop in the bull's hole, a muddy paddock on the edge of the English village. Some fifty people were already waiting, gawking, eager to help if they could.

"Landing's a delicate procedure, Jon," said my Dad. "One rip from a branch and the whole thing's ruined."

I looked at him, impregnable in his unchallengable certainty in everything he said. People were already taking the ropes to hold the balloon steady. I wanted to go forward and help. Its surface rippled—it was deflating, losing its solidity as the air inside cooled.

Ten, that age balanced between childhood and adolescence, like a space in which to draw breath before making a dive. I was already restless, lying awake on the light summer evenings listening to the rooks. The distant percussion of a fast train was a familiar sound—approaching, passing, fading. Always the same and therefore lulling. Destination seemed more than a word. It was the world. The world outside the village.

I always knew I was going to leave.

We used to go to the Natural History Museum, Dad and I. Get the train to Paddington and then the Underground. That was my favourite part of the trip, the narrow, curving tunnels and the machine noises of the escalators. The lost pigeons fluttering down from the iron girders of the roof. The journey was almost better than the museum itself, with its echoey halls and subdued hubbub of visitors come to see the fossil dinosaur bones or the life-size blue whale. Dad wouldn't say much. We'd wander round and then find the café where he'd have a slice of cherry cake and a cup of tea. Me perched on a stool beside him, sucking orange juice from a deflating carton.

Once, when I was five or six, I ran ahead in the tunnel that leads from the Circle line to the museum. But somehow I missed the exit and when I came out I didn't know where I was. I went back down the concrete stairs and retraced my steps but couldn't see where I'd gone wrong. I ran along the tunnel from end to end but it was as though the museum exit had never been there and I couldn't find my Dad either. There was a feeling of panic at being lost. At being lost to my Dad.

And then suddenly there he was, coming round the curve of the tunnel, walking just the way he always did.

My great uncle was found on a train. Too young to know his last name or where he lived. His real parents put him on the train to Manchester and, in one stroke, had one less mouth to feed. Our family found him.

That's our legend—a toddler found on a train. Somewhere there's a family with a story of a toddler lost on a train.

"I proposed to your mum on a station." It's rare that Dad lets slip anything about the past before I was born. The past is theirs, not mine.

"Which one?" I'm fifteen and curious.

"Oh Crewe probably."

I imagine the dirty grey platform of Crewe station, the smell of diesel, the noise. Crewe itself—an ugly place no one ever visits except to change trains.

"Why there?"

"Why not?" he says grumpily. Looking back now I can almost hear him thinking, *What does it matter where, compared to twenty-five years of marriage?*

Odd how these scraps of conversation stay with you when you forget so much else. I do remember him sitting back in his vast chair, feet up, full of Sunday lunch. Eyes closed, one hand tapping to the rhythm of an Ellington tune.

"Dad, why d'you like jazz?" I wanted to know.

"I just do," he said curtly.

At the time, I took this refusal to answer as an expression of contempt and searched for what I'd done wrong. Now, I don't know. Maybe I was afraid to admit that he couldn't answer.

I learned not to ask questions.

East of the village, a longer bridge steps its brick arches across the Thames, carrying Brunel's railway from Bristol to London. The track is eight level veins of iron, slotted through hills, raised up when the land drops away to maintain the horizontal speed of the trains. The non-stop trains would tear through our station like a crashing, endless bullet and I would hide in the stairwell shining with fear while it smashed past en route to London, dragging the air in its wake like a wind. If you stood too close, would you get sucked under?

I collected fragments of my parents' past as I got older but the pieces didn't always fit—misremembered, curled by time. Every witness had their own jigsaw.

What I wanted was one complete picture that everybody could agree on.

Dad shook my hand awkwardly the day I left, at seventeen. His fingers were bigger and rougher than mine, his shoulders broader. He was his father's son, could easily have worked on the trawlers like grandad if he'd needed to.

Mum smiled and cried a little, before the train shunted to a stop and the doors clattered open.

"Look after yourself," she said. Speaking rapidly in a lower voice just for me she added, "Don't mix your drinks. And don't have sex unless it's part of a serious relationship."

She stepped back. I climbed on board and swung the door shut. Slid the window down to wave. In sixty seconds we were crossing the bridge over the Thames.

Repeating that first solo journey to London, almost twenty years later, I catch sight of myself in the toilet mirror. My face, as I sway with the acceleration of the train, is more like his now. (Before, it was my mother's face.) I recognize his calm solidity, that same superficial appearance of strength.

The steady rhythm under the floor gives the sensation of standing on a platform that is flying past fields and satellite towns. Thicker, thicker the houses and warehouses, offices and yards. London's brown ugliness takes us in and then turns its back on us—graffitied walls, narrow windows of houses backing on to the train line. We pass an above ground Tube station—Royal Oak? It is crowded. The strangers hurrying through the veins of the city are its pulse, its promise.

There are questions that I would ask my Dad but I believe he doesn't have the answers. There is one important question. It is this.

I am on a train. It is a train that does not stop. It is going to the city where she lives. When I arrive in the city I have to make a decision. I have to say yes, and in that yes there is everything, or no.

The train is accelerating. There are no stops before the city.

There is a statue of a man in division 71 of Père-Lachaise cemetery in Paris. I found it by chance while walking along the cobbled paths, buckled by tree roots. This is what it is like.

His bronze thumb gleams like newly cast metal. It is cool to the touch, smooth. He lies on his back, offering his open hand, thumb projecting outward. As you step up to the tomb it is natural to grasp it to steady yourself. Holding his hand, poised on the narrow step, you find yourself looking down into his bearded face and the underwater calmness of his expression. His bronze skin has oxidized turquoise like something drowned in the sea, and rainwater has collected in the tarnished folds of his clothes with the dead leaves and the dirt. Only his golden brown thumb shines in the sun.

As you balance on the step you can also see his companion stretched out next to him. Clean-shaven, also in 19th century clothes, his face turned away from the path as though considering some private matter. He is not generously offering his strength and protection like the first, but he has the same air of tranquility and stillness.

Hot air balloonists, they ascended together to an altitude of 8,600 metres in 1875. This is so far from the ground that the thinning air gives out, but of course nobody in Paris knew that then. Euphoric from oxygen deprivation, they would have lost consciousness.

Standing gingerly by their side, holding onto his thumb, you can see that they too are holding hands. Their fingers are interlocked, something invisible from the path. It is the only statue I have ever seen of two men holding hands.

I get off the train.

Illuminations

Let us dig our furrows in the fields of the commonplace.

—Jean Henri Fabre

Waking Up in Notre-Dame

Christina Ammon

Sell your cleverness and buy bewilderment

—Jelaluddin Rumi

WHAT WAS IT ABOUT THIS WOMAN? Her perfectly tied scarf? Her posture? Her easy, but sage, eye contact? She certainly wasn't blustery and loud. She didn't dominate dinner tables, or command attention. Whatever it was, it couldn't be mimicked. It was a presence. A subtle gravity that drew your attention like a whisper. Something earned.

I had been invited to help teach a writing workshop at Shakespeare and Company. One of the students, Ann, wanted to work more deeply on her essay, and so we agreed to meet at a café near the bookstore one afternoon before class.

She breezed in at 4 p.m. sharp, unbuttoned her overcoat, straightened her scarf, and sat with her notebook. She carried the smell of crisp autumn leaves.

I got into my teacher frame-of-mind, slightly astonished to find myself in this position—as The Teacher—especially so with someone like Ann, who is a couple of decades older than me, who has trained airline pilots, and who has a poise and an aura of kindness that I've always aspired to. So, often while Ann studied writing, I studied Ann.

We ordered hibiscus tea, and I spread out my notes and got started. Ann lost her daughter to cancer several years ago, and her essay was about a healing retreat on an island. It was an articulate and heartfelt piece of writing, but like most first drafts, needed a bit of reordering and clarifying.

"I think it would be best if you reveal one spiritual lesson per section," I said, numbering each statement of revelation and circling the pertinent text.

It felt odd to reduce her enormous experience of grief into perfunctory writing tips. But I was a writer, not a psychologist. All I had were these tools of expression—the mechanics of sentence and sentiment. So, I continued.

". . . and, also, break down broad statements into precise details."

This was key. First drafts are so often fraught with words that bulge like overstuffed suitcases: *Anger. Beauty. Happy.*

Vivid writing is a trick of proportions. The writer has to get specific in order to communicate what is universal. As the saying goes, "God is in the details."

And so rather than say "the man was handsome," show us the arch of his brow, the lilt of his low voice. Don't tell us you were fed up with urban living. Show us yourself hurling your iPhone at the IKEA lamp across the room while a loud delivery truck blares its horn outside the window.

I circled the general words in Ann's essay and prescribed breaking them down into specific images.

When our meeting was over, I buttoned my coat and stepped back out into the streets. I crossed the bistro-lined street and followed it over the choppy Seine toward Notre-Dame. I'd passed the famed cathedral dozens of times, as awed as anyone by the flying buttresses which, depending on the light, looked by turns beautiful or sinister. But I'd never felt a particular need to go in, always too put off by the crowded entrance.

However, in that evening's dimming light, there was an unusual sense of spaciousness around the cathedral, and an easy flow of people going through the front door. I left the hint-of-winter air and yielded to the current. The atmosphere was full of hymns and incense. Mass was in session.

In just a few steps, I felt the sudden awe of taking that last step onto a mountain peak. Not a particularly religious sensation—in fact, it felt much deeper than religion. It was a rapping in the epicenter in my chest, that place sometimes stirred awake by poetry, or music. It was a sense of grandeur that sometimes jars me and makes me realize that, in fact, I spend most of my waking life numb and asleep.

I was happy to be there on my own with no brilliant and hilarious friend at my side to share whispering snarky invectives against religion, or running commentaries on the gothic architecture. Cathedrals, I realized, are best experienced alone.

I proceeded around the perimeter of the cathedral, past paintings, past alcoves, past the transept, under the arches, past people lighting candles, people kneeled in prayer, people gazing up, and felt myself in the presence of something very, very old. I was dwarfed, not just by the cavernous arches, but by time, too—by the old incantations, mysterious, inscrutable, perennial, and hallowed, reaching through the ages to me right there in my tennis shoes.

In that resounding space, I felt myself a detail, tiny but telling. This sense of proportion came to me as a relief, a break from the daily grind of trying to be Somebody.

Like a singular blade of grass in a large field, I was a working part of a larger order, and humbled by this mystery. Who was I in the grand scale of time and history?

I was small on the outside, but big on the inside—right in the place where good writing comes from.

I completed my wander around the cathedral and in one step entered again the small-mindedness of the street. My hallowed self started dozing off to sleep, and soon I was smoothing my hair in a shop window and craving a glass of house red.

I thought of Ann's loss, the size of it, and how it must constantly alter her own sense of scale; grief itself is an immense and sacred space. I thought of her calm presence, which was not out of timidity or shyness I now realized, but sourced from an inner life as vast as Notre-Dame.

Word Embers

Amy Marcott

AT TWO P.M., JUST AS I'D zipped up my coat, it started happening. My knees buckled, and I fell into the nearest chair, spent, as if I'd endured the entire day in a strong wind. Depression steeped like tea into my blood and drained through me, snaking down my limbs. This had been happening every day like clockwork for weeks, and I knew there was nothing I could do to stop it.

I'd recently earned my MFA in the States, and had built a creative momentum by spending hours writing in cafés. I felt at home sitting with a cup of tea writing in my journal and revising my novel, lulled by the din. In cafés, I found portals to that meditative space where words and sometimes entire stories flashed into my mind as if by magic, one sentence after another. I wrote without thinking, as if a car in the fast lane, with nothing obstructing me.

When I read what I'd written, it often surprised me and helped me understand my true feelings. Writing was how I made sense of life.

But soon depression extinguished my creative fire. Even if I tried writing early in the day, I could at best eke out a few scattered words in my journal, and repeatedly rewrite the same opening three paragraphs of my novel with only slight modifications.

I stopped perceiving the world as a writer. Snatches of dialogue or compelling descriptions that I'd previously seized for future narratives failed to pique my interest. My imagination was cold ash. I didn't know who I was or where I belonged.

I spent a lot of time staring at my walls, often at a painting I'd bought on a trip to Paris two months earlier. I'd read Hemingway's *A Moveable Feast*, and was struck by how artists in Paris had supported one another. Gertrude Stein and Ezra Pound had filled their apartments with the works of up-and-coming painters, and I took Stein's advice to Hemingway—"either buy clothes or buy pictures"—to heart. I didn't just want a painting, I *needed* it to connect me to these artistic souls.

One warm, June afternoon in the shadow of Sacré Cœur, Montmartre's Place du Tertre had the air of festival, with many easels set up and tourists encircling the *carré aux artistes*. Sunlight snuck past the trees and colorful umbrellas, dappling the canvases.

The present can be overwhelming in the Place du Tertre, with so many hasty charcoal portraits, even hastier caricatures. Pop-Art Eiffel Towers. Knock-off Impressionistic Pont Neufs.

Dripping ice cream cones and strains of accordion music and racks of postcards creaking when spun. People speaking English and German and Japanese thronging the cafés steps away.

I focused instead on the past. The soot-blackened corners of the 18th-century buildings made me feel like one of Victor Hugo's characters, feeling the soft-hewn wear of the cobblestones through thin shoes, the gunpowder of revolution in the air.

I navigated the square twice, dismayed that nothing seemed original. And then, as if conjured, an oil painting depicting a café scene appeared in front of me.

The artist had used smears and bursts of color: scarlet and persimmon, cobalt and jade, infused with luminous patches that bordered on the abstract. Only under scrutiny did I notice people and chairs and shadowy spirits traversing the background. My eye was drawn to an incandescence over a small table in the foreground. Two ghost-like women sat together, one shadowed in blues, the other bright with green and rust. Because the source of light was unseen, the glow above the table assumed its own presence. The way one woman leaned into it and the other was illuminated by it, the light seemed to me like possibility itself.

I knew I could not leave Paris without this painting.

"*Vous êtes l'artiste?*" I asked the woman sitting nearby. She was in her forties, petite, with dark hair and pale skin, a silk scarf, and a pursed-lip look of persistence. I could envision her sipping pastis in a café, watching the interplay of colors as the sun shifted.

"*Oui*," she said.

"*Combien*?" I pointed to the painting. It was 250e. A splurge, but I felt I would somehow be doing this trip an injustice if I didn't buy it. For years, I had lived in rooms with posters of Paris upon the walls, and now I wanted a genuine souvenir that meant I'd been there. I feared I might never return, and would feel an unrequited pang if I didn't buy this.

My French wasn't strong enough to ask the artist more about her connection to cafés, but I didn't need to. The way the scene floated on the canvas like a lovely, indistinct memory told me we felt the same way about them. Or felt the same way *in* them: that the world became a dreamy blur where anything could happen.

Still, I wanted her to know my affinity for these sacred spaces. "*J'aime les cafés aussi*," I said. "*J'écris là.*" I pantomimed writing. She asked me what I wrote and I said *un roman*, because I couldn't remember how to say short stories or fiction and I *had* just finished my novel draft.

After I paid, she led me up a narrow staircase to an apartment overlooking the square where she'd wrap my souvenir. Paintings leaned against the walls in thick stacks. Other canvases hung on a clothesline. Her productivity enthralled me. I hadn't yet published any stories, and my novel needed significant revision, but this was what I wanted: to sustain my creative momentum and write something to share with the world.

Paris summoned an artist's talent, and just as the undiscovered van Gogh shifted his palette from heavy browns to brighter, Impressionistic hues while in the city, I felt that

I would be a better writer for having been in Paris. I felt I'd purchased membership into the lineage of Parisian artists who found and supported one another, like the young Hemingway, who crossed paths with Joyce, Picasso, and Fitzgerald and who agreed to earmark some of his meager earnings to free T. S. Eliot from his bank job.

I couldn't know then how much I myself would need this.

Soon after I returned to the States, depression consumed me. Any amount of writing struck me as too daunting. I couldn't concentrate long enough to form a coherent paragraph. Words felt like cold, distant stars. I couldn't read a book and found music grating. My doctor said it would take months for the antidepressants to work, and I felt as if I were waiting for the Messiah all the while battling panic attacks and side effects: dizziness, insomnia *and* drowsiness, tremors that prevented me from lifting cups to my mouth without spilling.

Finally, the medication started to kick in and whittle away at my emotional numbness, and one day as I stared at the painting, I remembered that I'd previously been captivated by the glowing patches. This time I was struck by the shadowed woman in the foreground, the only figure with eyes, nose, *and* mouth, with a prominent swath of blue the color of a bruise on her back. The light in the painting didn't seem to create her shadow; rather, she carried it with her. Yet she radiated serenity and grace the way she leaned forward, her face and one closed eyelid just starting to catch the luminosity emanating from the table.

She wouldn't be in shadow for long and she knew it.

Overseeing her from the background is a half-shaded figure, possibly hooded, that struck me as the spirit of divine inspiration itself, just waiting to come out fully into the light. Now, the incandescent table seemed a beacon, reminding me that the enchanted zone I was currently denied access to still existed. It was there for the artists on the Place du Tertre, there for Hemingway with his pencils and notebooks in the Closerie des Lilas.

You will find your way back here, it seemed to be saying to me.

So I sat writing in cafés, though at most I'd write two paragraphs of stilted sentences before my attention drifted.

One rainy November night, I went to a café I'd avoided because it was usually mobbed with students. Soft yellow light warmed the interior, and strains of Indie folk music and wafts of newly-brewed espresso greeted me. I ordered a latte and sat near the window, reveling in the simple pleasure of warming my hands around a steaming mug.

When I opened my notebook, instead of rehashing old sentences, I wrote about the geometric designs and portraits à la Toulouse-Lautrec decorating the small tables. The whirring whoosh of the milk frothers. The lights shining through the windows from trams sliding along the slick tracks. The spine of staircase visible in the classroom building across the street.

My table's glazed surface gleamed from the overhead light, and a warmth extended from my cheeks down my neck. As my hand glided along the page, words landed like embers, and I knew they would spark stories.

Inside the Lie of Paris

Excerpt from *A Master Plan for Rescue*

Janis Cooke Newman

My novel, A Master Plan for Rescue, *is about the stories we tell ourselves—for good and for ill. There are two main point of view characters: Jack, a twelve-year-old boy in WWII New York City; and Jakob, a twenty something Berlin Jew.*

This excerpt is from Jakob's point of view. It is the late 1930s, and one by one, Hitler is taking away every privilege the Jews possess, including the right to teach Germans—the profession of Rebecca, the woman Jakob loves.

Unlike Jakob, Rebecca has a clear-eyed view of the Nazis' plans for them. The only lie she tells herself is that she will live long enough to escape Germany and go to Paris.

THAT WINTER, REBECCA advertised for private students. But no private students were willing to learn French from a Jew, and Rebecca had no one with whom to speak French except herself.

And that turned the lie ravenous.

On a frigid night near the end of January, I came home from the shop and found Rebecca wrapped in blankets on the sofa. The heat in the building was unpredictable and she'd forgotten to light the fire in the tiled stove, which we used for a back up. It was nearly as cold inside as out, yet her face was flushed and feverish-looking.

"When I go to Paris," she said, as I stepped through the door. Not, hello. Not, why are you late? Because I was late. Because five minutes before closing time, an officer of the Gestapo had come into the shop with a broken gramophone, and you do not tell an officer of the Gestapo that it is five minutes before closing time and would you mind very much coming back tomorrow. Not if the name on the door of your shop has a Semitic ring to it. No, you bow your head as if you are grateful for the business, and you accept the gramophone, and you stay as long as it takes to fix it, and then you arrive home late.

"The first place I go will be the Sorbonne," Rebecca was saying, as I built the fire. "And I will sit there until Giselle Freund agrees to see me."

"Is there food?" I asked her. "Have you thought about supper?"

"I will explain that I too, have escaped Hitler, and that even though she does not know me, she does. Then I will show her my photographs."

"Stay here. I will go and see if the butcher on Fraenkelufer is still open."

The butcher's shop was shuttered, and I had to resort to making a watery soup from what I could find at the bottom of our vegetable box. I do not believe Rebecca noticed. She barely stopped talking long enough to put the spoon in her mouth, hardly ceased speaking long enough to swallow.

She told me about the photographs Giselle Freund had taken for *Life* magazine, pictures she had heard of in rumor, because the Nazis would never have allowed *Life* magazine into Germany. "She has put photographs of the poorest of England's working class in the middle of a story on the British aristocracy," she told me, soup spilling down her chin. "She will understand my woman with the shriveled leg leaning against Josef Wackerle's concrete thigh."

While I tried to get her to eat the sorry soup, she explained how Giselle Freund would take her to meet all of her bohemian friends—Jean-Paul Sartre, who Rebecca claimed was never cheerful, and Colette, who she believed always was. She told me this in such detail that I saw it all inside my head, the way I saw how mechanical objects worked, and I began to believe in it myself. Only when her voice became hoarse and started to crack, did I remember that this was her lie.

I took the empty spoon out of her hand. "It's late," I said. "You can tell me the rest tomorrow."

Rebecca did. She told me about Paris the next day, and the day following. Until I realized that she never went out, never left the flat, only moved from the bed to the sofa, where she waited for me to come home from the shop so she could begin talking.

"When I go to Paris, I will live in the Latin Quarter on the rue St. Jacques, and I will have an apartment where all the windows face west and south, and none of them face east, so I will never have to look toward Germany."

"Rebecca, have you eaten today?"

"I will invite over all the people I have met there, all the people Giselle Freund has introduced me to. James Joyce and Jean Cocteau. Marcel Duchamp and Virginia Woolf."

"Let's go around to the café that serves the sheep stew you like."

"In Paris, I will eat *coq au vin,* and *cassoulet,* and *steak frites*, and I will eat them in any café I wish. Because no one on the Boulevard Saint Germain or rue de Rivoli or the Champs-Élysées will care that I am a Jew or an existentialist or a Hindu or a lesbian."

"Are you planning on becoming a lesbian in Paris?" I smiled.

"I might. In Paris, I might become something different everyday. A lesbian on Monday, a Negress on Tuesday, a devout Catholic on Wednesday. In Paris, I shall become whatever I want and there won't be a single Nazi to tell me that I can't because a quota for it has already been filled."

"And what about me?"

"You?" She wrapped a thin arm around my neck. "You, my darling, will come and fix the typewriters and cameras and bicycles of all my famous bohemian friends. Because of course, they are artists and incapable of fixing anything for themselves. And they will adore you and call you *indispensable*, which of course, you will be."

Listening to Rebecca talk was like falling into an opium dream. It was much easier to stay with her inside the lie of Paris than to go outside into the reality of Berlin. But I saw how the lie was feeding off her. How purpled the skin beneath her eyes had turned—a color I could not blame on the early sunsets of February. And at night, after the nervous energy of feeding the lie had finally exhausted her, I would reach under the sweaters she wore to bed and count her ribs with my fingers, a task that got easier each time I tried it.

Shakespeare and Co
PARIS, FRANCE

"On a cold windswept street, this was a lovely, warm, cheerful place..."
— Ernest Hemingway

Portraits

If you are strangers in Paris, we invite you to explore our Aladdin's cave for bibliophiles . . . in the Old Smoky Reading Room you can sit by the window overlooking the left bank of the Seine and Notre-Dame and enjoy the hospitality of the Mistral girls who offer you iced tea in summer and hot coffee in winter.
—1950s poster for The Mistral Bookshop, the original name of Shakespeare and Company

January in Paris

Billy Collins

A poem is never finished, only abandoned.

—Paul Valéry

That winter I had nothing to do
but tend the kettle in my shuttered room
on the top floor of a pension near a cemetery,

but I would sometimes descend the stairs,
unlock my bicycle, and pedal along the cold city streets
often turning from a wide boulevard
down a narrow side street
bearing the name of an obscure patriot.

I followed a few private rules,
never crossing a bridge without stopping
mid-point to lean my bike on the railing.

and observe the flow of the river below
as I tried to better understand the French.

In my pale coat and my Basque cap
I pedaled past the windows of a patisserie
or sat up tall in the seat, arms folded,
and clicked downhill filling my nose with winter air.

I would see beggars and street cleaners
in their bright uniforms, and sometimes
I would see the poems of Valéry,
the ones he never finished but abandoned,
wandering the streets of the city half-clothed.

Most of them needed only a final line
or two, a little verbal flourish at the end,
but whenever I approached,
they would retreat from their ashcan fires
into the shadows—thin specters of incompletion,

forsaken for so many long decades
how could they ever trust another man with a pen?

I came across the one I wanted to tell you about
sitting with a glass of rosé at a café table—
beautiful, emaciated, unfinished,
cruelly abandoned with a flick of panache

by Monsieur Paul Valéry himself,
big fish in the school of Symbolism
and for a time, president of the Committee of Arts and Letters
of the League of Nations if you please.

Never mind how I got her out of the café,
past the concierge and up the flight of stairs—
remember that Paris is the capital of public kissing.

And never mind the holding and the pressing.
It is enough to know that I moved my pen
in such a way as to bring her to completion,

a simple, final stanza, which ended,
as this poem will, with the image
of a gorgeous orphan lying on a rumpled bed,
her large eyes closed,
a painting of cows in a valley over her head,

and off to the side, me in a window seat
blowing smoke from a cigarette at dawn.

Interview with Filmmaker Gonzague Pichelin
Portrait of a Bookstore as an Old Man and *Love Letters* Project

Portrait of a Bookstore as an Old Man *is such an intimate portrait of George Whitman. How did the idea for the film originate and how did you acquire such open access to daily life at Shakespeare and Company?*

I first had the idea, then I met Benjamin Sutherland in Paris. He told me that he had worked at Shakespeare for more than two years, offering an all-round service, being cashier (a privilege), and above all getting to know George Whitman better. Benjamin, then, was the best gateway to the shrine.

Describe a typical day at Shakespeare and Company during George's reign.

The bookstore was like a swarm in a hive. With a flood of urban buzzing, visitors went in and out of the shop. George was the Queen Diva among his people. He enjoyed barking at customers and charming girls. He sponsored Monday evening poetry readings, cosmopolitan Sunday tea-parties and, during summer, dinner parties on the sidewalk out front. Guests repaired sagging shelves, tended the till, lugged books, mopped the floor with newspapers, spotted shoplifters, threw parties and made soup or love . . .

George fancied himself a **frère** *lampier, patterned after a medieval monk whose duty it was to light the lamps at nightfall. In what way do you think he lived this out?*

The shop was open late at night, until midnight. It was (and still is) the beacon for those drifters, poets, dharma bums, students, writers and readers in search of a literary shelter. And George was masquerading as a shepherd.

What did you learn from George?

To not be patient, ever.

Sylvia, George's daughter, now runs the bookshop. What do you think has changed and what remains the same?

She has gently but firmly cleaned the dust off the old shelves, revived the decaying building, and managed to reinvigorate the soul of the shop.

Where has the film been shown and how can we see it?

Almost everywhere in the world except the Middle East and China. It was shown on Sundance Channel in prime-time for two years. We have DVDs, which you can order at gonzague. pichelin@gmail.com

What new projects are you working on?

The Love Letters Project. In the summer of 2000, a handsome thirty-six-year-old single Parisian posed (clothed) for a full-page photograph in a popular, large-circulation French woman's magazine. Readers desiring a romantic relationship were invited to read an interview with the man and write him, care of the magazine, with details of their lives and romantic aspirations. one hundred eighty-five single women replied. Each letter was a manifestation, often powerful, of female desire. The bachelor was me. I was overwhelmed and decided to not meet a single woman.

Some of the sheets of paper, parchments and envelopes had been sprayed with perfume, painted with watercolors. One envelope contained a stick of still-fragrant incense. The collection includes a large selection of stamps affixed to envelopes for replies. The letters, many containing poems, drawings or photographs, were written in France, save a dozen or so penned in Belgium, Canada, Costa Rica, Denmark, Germany, Latvia, Spain and Switzerland. The letters embody France's strong epistolary tradition, which greatly values detailed expressions of sentiments, romantic recollections and beautiful penmanship. (Only ten of the letters are typewritten; one is partially typed.)

Each letter was written to a man who had been introduced with just a single photograph and short interview, so the letters reveal their authors far more than the addressee. Written to an abstraction, they apply to an archetype of man—and therefore all men.

This ongoing project includes an art installation of the letters and a film which highlights the women, and casts light on the masculine ideal as an archetype constructed and modified since time immemorial in the minds of women, the meaning of the letters as well as their place in Western *correspondance amoureuse*, from medieval texts of chivalric romance and courtly love to today's love letters and digitally-expressed sentiments.

The Rarest of Editions[2]

Erin Byrne

There is something gorgeous about him, some heightened sensitivity to the promises of life.

—F. Scott Fitzgerald, *The Great Gatsby*

IF BOOKS ARE HUMANITY in print, he's the king of the world.

The old man sits holding his worn paperback. His gnarled fingers, veins raised under papery skin, caress the cover as if it were an archaeological treasure he has just unearthed in the deserts of Egypt. His thin plaid-flannel-shirted frame hunches on a low stool, knobby knees sticking up at awkward angles. He sits majestically in his small but stately palace.

---

2   Editor's note: This story was written in 2010, the year before George Whitman died.

His rheumy eyes rise to contemplate his kingdom: a tiny set of rooms lit by dusty chandeliers, crammed floor to ceiling with books. He observes his subjects: an assortment of characters whose eyes glaze over with the wonder of being among thousands of new, old and rare editions. He savors the sounds of his domain: pages shuffling, pure-pleasure sighs, the murmur of voices, the clattery squeak of the door as it opens, and the nearby bells of Notre-Dame.

He lifts his head with its long strands of silky white hair and inhales the comforting scent of that magical combination of books and people: leather, paper, ink and interest. The promising perfume of historical, imaginary and fantastical lives. The smell that makes one instantly settle in for a good read.

A girl with short dark hair and berry lips sinks down cross-legged against the Poetry shelf. Her black eyes race across the page as she whispers. A graying professor grabs *Ulysses* and curls up to it while standing. A bleary-eyed traveler breathes in the limb-loosening smell of home and dives into *The World Atlas* to plan the next leg of his journey.

The old man smiles, releasing a wreath of leatherish wrinkles and thinks: *A stranger walking the streets of Paris can believe he is entering just another of the bookstores along the left bank of the Seine, but if he finds his way through a labyrinth of alcoves and cubbyholes and climbs a stairway leading to my private residence then he can linger there and enjoy reading the books in my library and looking at the pictures on the walls of my bedroom.*

Such is the welcoming spirit of George Whitman, proprietor of Shakespeare and Company bookstore in Paris.

George spent time in his youth wandering through South America and the generous hospitality of the locals burrowed its way into his soul. When he found himself in Paris at the end of the war, he enrolled at the Sorbonne and began building his legendary book collection inside his hotel room on Boulevard Saint Michel. He invited booklovers to come browse his library of English translations and walk out, beaming, with a literary treasure or two. George's reign of bringing people to books began.

Shakespeare and Company is snuggled inside a little green-painted shop on the rue de la Bûcherie with the Seine so close it nearly runs through it, across from Notre-Dame. *When I opened my bookstore in 1951, this area in the heart of Paris was a slum with street theatre, mountebanks, junkyards, dingy hotels, wine shops, little laundries, tiny thread and needle shops and grocers,* George wrote in his bookstore's brochure-booklet-manifesto. He's always considered himself a modern version of the *frère lampier*, the sixteenth century monk whose job it was to light the lamps outside the building, then a monastery.

For sixty years, George has provided a sanctuary for writers and artists, whom he calls "tumbleweeds." This is the creed of the tumbleweed*: Give what you can and take what you need.* He invites all to stay in his house provided they read a book a day and put in a few hours at the cash register. These young, bright-eyed literary angels float around fingering, adjusting, straightening. They lean against the display table and fervently recommend their favorites. They discuss authors with the air of heirs to the throne. *We wish our guests to enter with the feeling they have inherited a book-lined apartment on the Seine which is all the more delightful because they share it with others.*

George, at ninety-seven years old, is now retired and only descends from his upstairs lair to grab a book, greet a guest, or wave to his minions. His daughter, Sylvia, a young woman in her early thirties, swirls through the shop in a pretty skirt and blond ponytail with the poise of a prima ballerina.

Sylvia orchestrates the constant stream of literary events held outside on the sidewalk under the Parisian blue sky, or in George's own private library upstairs which includes books once held in hands that penned the classics of modern literature—Graham Greene, Jean-Paul Sartre, Simone de Beauvoir and others. Their spirits linger to listen and loosen tongues at the poetry readings and writer's gatherings that bring strangers shoulder-to-shoulder, hip-to-hip, on the benches that line the walls. A trip up the narrow staircase at the back of the store brings the visitor face-to-face with furrowed brows, heads bent over scratching pens, or giggling children squeezed together on the floor eager for a story. An advertisement for a recent event captures the mood that resides in the room atop the rickety stairs:

> Tonight Shakespeare and Company launches **Bard-sur-Seine**. We're planning to live up to our name by staging readings of the great Bard's plays hosted by **Leslie Dunton-Downer** and **Alan Riding,** authors

of *The Essential Shakespeare Handbook*. The first play in the series will be *Twelfth Night*. **Please note: all the roles in this session of Bard-sur-Seine have now been filled. As there are only players and no audience in this special production, we ask that only those who have signed up attend.**

It is easy to imagine the Bard's ghost as the lone member of the audience, sitting up straight, hose-clad leg crossed, Elizabethan collar sticking out stiffly. George would peek out of his bedroom door and shuffle across the room in his slippers to join him, and they'd laugh themselves into stitches at some private joke.

In this age of eBooks, audio books, downloadable and virtual books, George holds steadfastly and single-heartedly to the rectangular real thing, which are scattered, staggered, and strewn about when they are not picked up, pored over or propped open.

These weathered books contain poetry the literary monarch knows by heart, heroes he has been, women he has loved, villains he has vanquished, and orphans he has rescued from the streets. They have taken him to countries he has dreamed of and lands he has conquered. As Nietzsche observed, books speak out the most hidden and intimate things to those who love them.

On the top shelf, toga-clad Socrates poses a question to bespectacled Sartre. Seneca flourishes his stylus and writes, *The good man possesses a kingdom*. Rumi rubs shoulders with the irreverent Rimbaud as the wine sings in their veins. *Gandhi's*

Autobiography sits straight and still upon *One Hundred Years of Solitude.* Miller spoons Nin. Gide, squeezed next to Gibbons, glances across the room and winks at Wilde. Pink paper-backed Nancy Mitford nestles next to Thomas Mann. Balzac and Tom Wolfe, thrown together unexpectedly, exchange ironic eye-rolls. Dumas challenges Dostoevsky to a duel. Dante burns, Vronsky seduces, Quixote shouts. Gavroche dances in the street.

The action floats out into the city of Paris. Right up the street, Hemingway and Fitzgerald putter in from their rainy, spirit-swilling road trip—the Renault crawls down rue Jacob. Across the river Quasimodo swings from the bells, and one can hear the guillotine clatter and slam as it slices the naked neck of Marie Antoinette. Simone de Beauvoir calmly sips a *café crème* up the hill at Les Deux Magots.

The bookstore's namesake boldly assures his company:

> *Not marble nor the gilded monuments*
> *Of princes shall outlive this pow'rful rhyme*

George Whitman loves books with a pure love—hardback, paperback, shiny-new, well-worn, leather bound, cloth bound. Many of them still hold his salty tears within their bindings. Some he has immersed himself in and then tossed lightly aside, some he has hurled from him with great force. Some he has read again and again. A few he has memorized. This elderly hero is convinced he is living inside a novel. Who can question this?

The most tantalizing books on these shelves are the ones he has never read. They are virgin territory, uncharted seas. Between their covers he may find the key to his heart or instructions on how to release his sword from its stone. They may hold the secret of the fountain of youth and make him live forever.

Henry Miller called Shakespeare and Company a wonderland of books. Allen Ginsberg enjoyed hanging out having tea with George, as have countless others. He has engaged in mind-bending conversations with both the famous *and* the starving writers who are guests in his castle. His brain has been rubbed and polished to a brilliant shine, even as age approaches its edges.

As George sits on his low stool cradling his precious book, a woman approaches and he gallantly offers his leafy hand. His face opens in welcome. George at once apologizes for his disheveled appearance, he says that usually these days he stays upstairs in his pajamas. The two discover they have a friend in common. "Ah, of course I remember, he stayed here!" The timbre of his voice belies his age as he politely inquires, "Are you a writer too?" When she nods, he invites her to stay for as long as she wants. She is more than welcome anytime she's in Paris, anytime at all.

The two discuss the book he's holding and the bond of two bibliophiles is fondly established. They share the anticipation that builds when the cover crinkles open to the first line on the first page. Both have tumbled over the waterfall-plunge into a story and found themselves engulfed in characters. They've travelled to the center of their own souls while buried between pages. Both know the heartbreaking finality of the last line on the very last page and the sinking feeling when the cover is closed. For a long moment, George and the woman stand smiling at each other.

It's clear that George Whitman has fashioned a life for himself that brings together the two things he loves most in all the world, books and people. This combination makes him tick. Old age without loneliness is unusual; George always has a house full of friends. Fragility without weakness is seldom seen; this man is thin and frail, but his presence is noble. He is the rarest of editions, a truly happy human being.

> *I may disappear leaving behind me no worldly possessions—just a few old socks and love letters, and my windows overlooking Notre-Dame for all of you to enjoy. And my little Rag and Bone Shop of the Heart, whose motto is: Be not inhospitable to strangers lest they be angels in disguise. I may disappear, leaving no forwarding address, but for all you know I may still be walking among you on my vagabond journey around the world.*

Every evening as George dims the lights, caresses one last book, and glides through his labyrinth as effortlessly as the cats that purr around his ankles, he has lived life to the fullest. He climbs the twisting stairs, bids a polite *Bonsoir* to the tumbleweeds, and then the old monarch lays his wispy-haired head upon the pillow and falls asleep in the lap of legends old.

George Whitman died December 14, 2011 at home in his rooms upstairs at Shakespeare and Company. I spent that fall as guest instructor of the Evening Writing Workshops, working with writers in the next room, George's private library, which he shared with everyone It was then that the stories in the original edition of Vignettes & Postcards *were written. The atmosphere he cultivated in his little bookshop wove its way into the hearts of writers for nearly sixty years, and is carried on by his daughter, Sylvia Whitman.*

In this and many ways, he lives on.

Vignettes & Postcards

Writings From the Evening
Writing Workshop at Shakespeare
and Company Bookstore, Paris
Original Edition (Fall 2011)

Enduring work follows from a leap into the void,
into unknown territory, icy water, or murderous rock.
—Fernand Pouillon, *The Stones of the Abbey*

Anything good that I have written has, at some point during its
composition, left me feeling uneasy and afraid. It has seemed,
for a moment at least, to put me at risk.
—Michael Chabon, *Maps and Legends*

FOREWORD
Erin Byrne

The only thing we are missing is angels. In this vast world there is no place for them. And anyway would our eyes recognize them? Perhaps we are surrounded by angels without knowing it.

—Henry Miller, quoted in *The Rag and Bone Shop of the Heart*, George Whitman's bookstore brochure

THE ROOM WAITS. VOICES and footsteps from the bookstore underneath echo in the empty space. Through an open window the buzz of traffic breezes in past pink geraniums which linger in their wooden box, savoring the last light of day. Dust motes circle in rhythm. An old table appears to have pushed aside a chess set on its own top to clear space for paper and pen.

This is George Whitman's private library at Shakespeare and Company Bookstore. For six decades, he presided at the cash register, shouted commands across the room at random strangers, invited many to tea or to stay, and swished between bookshelves. But now, in September of 2011, he lies in bed inside his apartment up the stairs, as life ebbs from his frail body. George's spirit still infuses the shop, but his is now a wispy presence.

The people clomp, stumble and tiptoe up the stairs. Collectively they read, write and speak in dozens of languages. They come from all over the world—Brazil, New Zealand, Ireland, Holland, Iran, Lebanon, and other places. Their communal consciousness overflows with precise details, harvested impressions and thriving ideas. On this warm evening, they came from all over Paris—on foot, on bicycles, on métro, on buses—to create something tangible out of the richness of their lives.

For three years, Anna Pook has been gathering with writers in this room. With her tawny hair and pink cheeks, she nestled in the corner, her back to the wall lined with signed editions of legendary writers. Anna spent weeks thumbing through piles of books, looking for excerpts that enticed her students to emulate the greats. She crafted prompts to loosen their pens. She learned each writer's interests, quirks and delights to cultivate an atmosphere of acceptance. Anna's gift of gentleness, combined with her unwavering insistence on honesty, inspired people to write stories, poems and essays that astonished even them.

But Anna has gone home for a few months to nurture her newborn daughter, and has invited me to serve as instructor for the fall session. To me, the room feels heavy with literary dignity, figures of the past float through the room, and Anna, in her thick gray cardigan, is one more ethereal image.

I sit in the library full of ghosts feeling the reality of this challenge. After several short seminars, this is my first lengthy workshop; my feet are on the precipice.

The room and I wait together.

People burst in, some out of breath, a few checking their phones, one woman rummaging through her bag. Anna's regulars have brought fresh-baked cookies and a bottle of wine, and tease each other with fond familiarity. Shy newcomers linger in the corner shadows. For a fleeting moment, I wish I could do the same.

They all settle in around the ridges of the room, and the crammed bookcases, musty cushions, and haphazard piles of books seem to shift to make space, inviting the writers in. Somehow this library lends encouragement.

The space grows quiet again. I feel the focus of experienced eyes and remember the advice from a mentor, former writer in residence (fondly called "tumbleweeds" here) Phil Cousineau.

"All you have to do," he said, "is coax their stories out of them."

I can only be myself, not some brilliant word-fairy.

So we begin. I have planned a seven week workshop, *Leaping Into the Void,* with a focus on taking risks in writing. The writers' first venture is to write vignettes inspired by whatever seizes them on a half-hour expedition inside the bookstore or outside in the surrounding area. It has been said that if you dig deep enough you will reach something universal, and these writers begin their excavations.

Claire Fallou, a young French woman with a delicate curve to her cheeks moves the chess set a little farther over and begins writing about the paving stones of Paris. Maria Bitarello, brow furrowing over sharp brown eyes, strains to remember the pained limp of a man she met while filming a documentary in Brazil. Philip Murray-Lawson's writing style rings with the same wit and mysterious intonations of his deep, Scottish voice. Jean-Bernard Ponthus gazes into the adjoining room and squints to see colorful scraps of paper tacked onto a mirror. Catalina Girón twists a strand of hair while imagining a vivid scene at a métro station.

Often, an elderly woman in a long skirt and boots flounces across the room, George's black dog, Colette, on her heels. "What are you all writing?" she asks, not waiting for an answer but disappearing through the door leading to George's apartment. After she's gone, we all exchange astonished looks. We have no idea who she is, but a hint of romance lingers in her wake. Another page in Shakespeare and Company's story, a postcard sent to us to add to the collection.

The sidewalks of Paris are lined with racks of postcards: sepia images of a grainy Louvre, black-and-white photographs of old men in berets, prints of Toulouse-Lautrec's cabaret dancers kicking up their petticoats. The writers create scenes drawn from one randomly chosen.

When the people read their work aloud, synchronicities occur. Karen Isère, dark hair swooping down over one eye, reads her poem about the majestic fragility of Notre-Dame, and bells from the cathedral chime as if on cue. Laura Orsal reads her story about a grieving woman weaving up toward this very room. She reaches the part when a young man begins to play the piano; and on the piano in the adjoining room, notes are plunked. Nancy Szczepanski pries open a foil-wrapped rectangle and, as she evokes her mother kneading and turning dough, the scent of cinnamon, sugar, and yeast fill the air.

As the stories take shape and are shared, they reflect the writers' own places, events, and characters, their own wit and mysteries and shadow sides. To me, the stories written in this room imbue something else as well: a combination of the past literary genius-ghosts whose musty signatures grace the books, George Whitman's once formidable but now hidden presence, Anna's nurturing, and whatever synchronicity caused those bells to peal and piano strings to vibrate.

There is a something *other* at work here, and it can be detected in the pages of this anthology. I invite you to find it in Martin Raim's passionate wooing of Lady Inspiration; in Jennifer Fleuckiger's vision of Homer and his pals scoffing at her from a cloud; in Manilee Sayada's trip inside Sylvia Plath's home on the night of her suicide.

Perhaps you will catch a glimpse of this quality in Rosemary Milne's character Leila, an Algerian woman on the outskirts of Paris, or in Emily Seftel's wry observations of people watching themselves watch the Mona Lisa, or in Julie Wornan's two waiters, frozen in time as if inside an ice cube.

I suppose we all call it something different: inspiration, brilliance, or simply good writing. I call it Real Work. Fernand Pouillon, the 20th century architect and writer, wrote that courage lies in being oneself, in loving what one loves and discovering the deep roots of one's feelings: *A work must not be a copy, one of a group, but unique, sound and untainted, springing from the heart, the intelligence, the sensibility. A real work is truth, direct and honest. It is simply a declaration of one's knowledge to the whole world.*

These writers cleared a space inside themselves—crushed internal censors, crawled out from under their own rigid expectations, and followed their instincts. They made room for their own Real Work to emerge. Look for the result in Sana Chebaro's view of a Degas painting, Leslie Lemon's street in 1950s Texas, Ann Dufaux's scene on rue de Seine during the flood of 1910, and Laura Mandel's depiction of her grandmother's last moments.

Find your own "something other" inside these stories, essays, poems, vignettes and postcards. You may even start to wonder what would happen if a story or two were coaxed out of you.

—Erin Byrne
Seattle, Washington, February 2012

Vignettes & Postcards First Edition was launched in Paris in May 2012 at an event in the upstairs library at Shakespeare and Company. The rooms were packed, with people scrunched on chairs without an inch to spare, crammed into the back room against The Mirror of Love, peering out from around the corner of the piano room, clustered at the top of the stairs in back, and through an open door, crowded on the side stairs and in the hallway that had led to George's apartment.

Tumbleweeds bustled about welcoming everyone, pouring wine, congratulating the writers, who read with unexpected flair: a Texan accent, a toss of the head, a voice pushing up through tears, a dramatic pause before an emphatic word. Something gave them an extra push . . . or someone.

George Whitman's physical body was gone, but his ghost leaned against the door-jam, his wiry hair springing out and bouncing as he nodded and clapped.

The room had waited a long time for this.

Inspiration

What are the best things and the worst things in your life,
and when are you going to get around to
whispering or shouting them?

—Ray Bradbury, *Zen in the Art of Writing*

Cinnamon Bread

Nancy Szczepanski

I grew up in the late sixties and early seventies, when Wonder Bread, Ding Dongs, and Mother's brand pink and white frosted animal cookies filled the cupboards of most American kitchens. Not at my house. My mother perfumed the air and filled the cookie jar and bread box with homemade babka, blueberry slices, snickerdoodles, and, my favorite, cinnamon bread.

The taste and texture of her cinnamon bread has always been a delicious solace to me, particularly when life is topsy-turvy, or completely upside down, as it has been this past year. In quick succession, I lost my father, left my job in hopes of pursuing a new career path, and my husband left me. The last event not only broke my heart, but also dashed my hopes of starting an entrepreneurial business. I grieved the loss of a parent, the loss of my beloved, and the loss of my dream.

Despite a diminished appetite, I craved the comfort of cooking. I leafed through my folder of family recipes and pulled out a spattered and crinkled sheet: Mom's Cinnamon Bread. As I lined up the ingredients on the counter, I sought refuge not just among the canisters and measuring spoons, but also in the warm memories of baking with my mom.

I watched my mother as she kneaded the dough: knead and turn, knead and turn, one quarter turn clockwise each time, her hand dipping into the flour canister and showering the wooden board with the white dust so the dough wouldn't stick. I sat beside her on a stool drawing letters and pictures with my finger in the flour.

Knead and turn, knead and turn, again and again, using the palm of her hand to push the dough away until it was smooth and supple, so cushiony-soft I wanted to lay my head down on it. She took out a large metal bowl and slathered it with butter, then plopped the dough inside, turning it over so both sides were glossy. She draped it with a bleached flour-sack tea towel and left it to nap.

Inch by inch, a pillow of dough puffed its head up over the rim of the bowl. I punched it down with a balled-up fist. Air whooshed out from the sides and the dough shrank back, as if frightened, into a deflated, wrinkled blob. Mom pinched off a piece for me, and I poked, rolled, squeezed and squished it between my fingers.

She divided the dough into three equal parts. Taking one piece at a time, she rolled her hands from the center outward, stretching the dough like a rubber band. It wriggled back, so she coaxed it again and again until it became a long, snaky rope. She whisked together cinnamon and sugar, a cloud of red-brown dust floating in the air as she whirled the two together on waxed paper. I licked the tip of my finger and dabbed it into the dune of sweet sand. The rough grains scratched the tip of my tongue and the roof of my mouth.

She gently braided the pliant ropes like she did my long blond hair, under, over, under, over, tucking under and pinching the ends. She plopped them into buttered tins, swaddling them with the cloth to protect them from the draft while they settled in for their second nap.

Again the dough grew and stretched like an inflating balloon until it reached the top of the pans. Mom slid the loaves into the hot oven and set the timer to ticking. The aromas of yeast, butter, and caramel tickled my nose and made my tummy grumble.

I waited.

The *brrrring* of the timer sent me running to the kitchen. Mom picked up the loaves with mitted hands and flipped them upside down; steam rose up from their backs as she removed the tins. She bent over the loaves with a tilted head, then tapped her fingers, one, two, three times, on the bottom. Like a doctor seeking the comforting thump, thump of a heartbeat, she listened for a hollow response. If the sound wasn't pleasing, she tipped the bread back into the pans and they disappeared for a few more minutes in the oven. When the loaves were finally done, she set them to rest right side up on a cooling rack.

I looked from the loaves to my mom with hungry eyes, but they were too hot to cut. I waited and waited for them to cool, distracting my impatience with my favorite TV shows: *Sesame Street, Mister Roger's Neighborhood, and Captain Kangaroo.*

Finally, she called from the kitchen. I clambered up the three wooden steps of the kitchen stool, tucked my legs under me, and folded my hands on the table. I watched as she sawed through the toasty-crisp shell into the creamy, feathery interior, revealing the swirling pinwheel of cinnamon sugar in the center. She cut thick slices and gave the still-warm bread a generous swipe of butter. It seeped into the pores, staining the bread yellow-gold. She sat down beside me at the table; together we raised the bread to our noses and inhaled. We looked at each other and smiled.

Now, decades later, I bite into the bread and the crust crunches. The butter oozes and its sharp saltiness mingles with the sweetness of the cinnamon sugar.

The taste and texture wrap around and hold me.

The Key to Many Doors

Rosemary Milne

I want to read and write so that I can stop being the shadow of other people.

— Paulo Freire

LEILA SITS DOWN AND the chair strains beneath her bulk.

"Hello. How are you? It's hot. I'm tired," she says in a single breath.

"Hello." says Marie, looking up. "Me too. I'm quite tired as well."

Leila smoothes her head scarf and sits for a moment, arms folded, gathered into herself. Marie is bent over her bag, shuffling through papers. Leila pushes up off the chair, muttering an "excuse me" as she leaves the room. She comes back with a wet cloth in her hand and begins wiping the coffee rings and bread crumbs off the table, strong, thick strokes, back and forth. She hums a little tune as she wipes the mess away. Once the surface is clean, she pushes the windows open.

"We need fresh air or we fall asleep."

Like the humming, this is more to herself than to Marie. She returns the cloth to the kitchen, pulls a book out of her bag, and presses the pages open. Her index finger edges along the line as she reads aloud, spelling out the words letter by letter: "*Pierre a sept ans. Il va à l'école. Il a deux soeurs . . .*" The other students file in and Marie starts the lesson.

Leila is in her usual place, facing Marie. Her dress is the same as always: a full-length, high-necked, loose garment in a dull gray-green, the headscarf of the same material. In repose the face framed by the scarf is severe and unrevealing. Marie is half Leila's age, a diminutive woman with the soft face of the young and untested. Despite her lack of experience she enjoys teaching the industrious Leila, the only one of the students who arrives on time with her homework done. But she is in terror of the noisy Leila, the one who constantly interrupts the others, and she goes cold inside when Leila starts up with her huffing and tutting as soon as Ahmed starts to speak. Ahmed, the only man in the class, has lived in France fifteen years but can barely string a coherent sentence together. Leila sees Marie's frowns, but she's unrepentant. As she tells the class at their first meeting, she has waited a long time to learn.

"I was born in a village high up in the mountains of Algeria. There, it is marriage and children for girls, never lessons. They say a wife's best teacher is her husband. I was a child of twelve years when I was married. Soon I have a baby and then more. Five altogether. All I know is shopping and cooking and mending and cleaning. Now is my chance. Now I shall read and write at last."

For most of the past forty years Leila has lived in the same building in that narrow slice of crowded streets and vacant lots that lies between the two great stations of northern Paris: *la Gare de l'Est and la Gare du Nord.* It's there that she and her husband have raised their children, sharing the four-room apartment with her mother-in-law and her husband's brother.

The Paris Leila knows is the opposite of the picture-postcard Paris. She is vocal in her dislike of the dog dirt and the litter but other details that might shock—even delight—an incomer pass unnoticed by her: the ebb and flow of multi-colored, polyglot humanity; the graffiti on every bare wall; half-finished housing projects; small shops open late, bundled sleeping shapes in doorways and under bridges; cafés stowed out with men—only ever men!—nursing their glasses of mint tea and strong coffee; the scents of spices, patchouli, jasmine; the African women in their bright cotton prints, selling maize cobs out of trolley bags; and the beggars with their battered cardboard cups and hands outstretched for alms.

This is her home and she swims in the crowded, muddy pond of it as a fish swims in the clear blue sea. She has her friendship networks, the weekly rhythm of the mosque and hammam, the market and the sewing circle to keep her busy. Why should she want more? The other women in the class nod in sympathy as she goes on with her story.

"My mother-in-law is a very strong woman. She says all the time to my husband, 'A good wife does not need books in French. What does your own mother read? Only the words of the Prophet, blessed be His name. This is enough for any woman.' So for all the time he never let me learn to read. But now he got tired. He wants me to do more than only clean and cook. So he changes his mind. His mother? Ha! She is still not happy, but he thinks now more about himself and not so much of what she says."

As the months go by, Marie learns to love this woman's determination and she is sorry when the term comes to an end. Months later, when they meet again by chance, she barely recognizes the older woman who greets her. Leila looks lighter and less care-worn. Her dress still matches her head scarf, but the dark blue of it is embroidered with red and gold. Leila embraces her teacher warmly and with a mischievous smile pulls out her house keys and jingles them at Marie.

"These keys? Same ones as my husband's. They open our house door." Marie nods, not understanding. "But—aha!" She snaps open her purse, "This key is only mine. Look, there is my name!" She plants a kiss on the library card she's taken out then slips the precious rectangle of blue and white plastic back safely inside her bag once more. She lays a hand on Marie's arm. "This key you gave me, and it opens many doors. . ."

Inspired Writing

Martin Raim

WALT BLITZER, CNN, REPORTING live from Paris. We're on the plaza of world-famous Notre-Dame, talking to fledgling writer Martin Raim. Martin, hundreds of tourists are milling about, and here you sit, tapping furiously on your laptop, immersed in what can only be . . . inspired writing!

Absolutely right, Walt. How on earth did you guess?

Reporter's instinct, Martin. Inspired writing is news these days. Rare as solar eclipses and abominable snowmen. The question our viewers keep asking is: Why doesn't every writer just put his mind to it and get inspired?

Because minds don't cooperate, Walt. I can't think my way to great prose, at least not with my mind calling the shots. He narrates, I type. He spots typos, I fix them. He orders rewrites, I acquiesce. It's chaos. And he critiques as I type. One minute it's *O God, pure nectar!* And the next, *You embarrass us, Martin, the publishers will puke!*

Then what's the secret of inspired writing?

A quiet mind, Walt. Simple as that.

Show us your opening paragraph, Martin.

Sure thing.

> 7 a.m. Heavy knocking. I stumble downstairs, open the front door. It's Weasel and Dwarf. Weasel's tall, pinch-faced, wrapped in a trench coat. Dwarf's hump-backed, one-eyed, dripping saliva. Weasel hands me his business card: Electricity Company of France! "Your house," he hisses, "uses too much power. More than a small factory. My employer is curious. A small house like yours. So much electricity. What's going on?" Dwarf tugs at his leash. "My colleague," whispers Weasel, "would like to come in and look around."

Martin, I'm hooked! Why doesn't everyone go mindless and write prose like that?

Because the mind does not surrender gladly. God knows, I tried. Five years on a mountaintop meditating with yogis. It looked like inner peace but under the surface it was pure hell, a spiritual free-for-all, my mind and me, punching, ear biting, hair pulling. I got lucky, floored him with a left jab to the super-ego. Bang! The internal monologue stopped mid-sentence. Blissful silence. I took a breath, made a wish, and Lady Inspiration tiptoed in. Within minutes, two short stories materialized. I was dizzy with opportunity, but she caught sight of Mind, groaning, sprawled on the floor. She burst into tears and fled.

Fled? But we caught you here in the throes of inspiration. How'd you get her back?

Negotiation, Walt. Mind eventually recovered; we shook hands and forged a non-aggression pact. I pushed through an Inspiration clause, guaranteed visiting rights and one hour of mindlessness per day. She spurned us! Years passed. Then, a few months ago, a moonlit night in Paris, I sensed her presence. Mind cleared out, and ever so gracefully she filled the vacuum, let her hair down, made herself comfortable. I dove right in: two stories and an essay. I was swept along in the tail of a comet aswarm with storylines, protagonists, monsters, metaphors, not to mention a myriad of tantalizingly mundane objects, shoe-laces, olive pits, electricity bills. Next I dashed off a piece on dental floss. The Creative Unconscious unleashed! And then. . .

And then?

Mind barged in, started reading over my shoulder. *This,* he said, *had better be good.* The scowl, which lasted page after page, vanished midway through "Ode to a Strand of Floss." Let's give the girl her due—she has wit. But "the girl" had long since fled.

Boy meets girl, boy loses girl. But you did win her back. Why here, Martin? Why Notre-Dame?

I'm on assignment, a seven-week inspiration workshop. Teacher tossed us out of the womb and gave us a deadline: twenty minutes to find Inspiration.

The womb?

My classroom, just across the Seine, the rickety building decked out in Christmas lights. It's the oldest English bookstore in Paris. Teacher's orders were: "Inspiration, do or die. Choose an author and meditate in front of his books." Inspiration by induction. I grabbed my laptop, ran downstairs and beat everyone to the Hemingway section.

Reunited with Inspiration. In front of Hemingway!

Far from it, Walt—all I got was visions of bullfights. I moved over to F. Scott Fitzgerald, but vanity and alcohol don't figure in my writing. Then Roth; you can't miss with Roth. I wrote like mad.

Inspired at last!

Not at all. Mind was in charge, wagging his finger—*Don't even think about showing this filth to your classmates. Do you think anyone cares how many times a day you . . .*

CNN viewers don't!

I could see myself slinking back to class, wilting with humiliation, uninspired and empty-handed. Then, praise God, the eight o'clock bells of Notre-Dame. A Proustian moment! I metamorphosed back into my nine-year-old self, a bookaholic immersed in *The Hunchback of Notre-Dame.* I came to, dashed out of the bookstore, crossed the bridge, grabbed this bench and beheld Notre-Dame, aglow, illuminated by hundreds of high intensity spotlights. *Who pays for all the electricity?* mused Mind, and then he withdrew.

Withdrew?

We had a binding agreement. Inspiration was in the air. Time was running out. I had to write, and it had to be inspired. That's what makes these workshops work: non-negotiable deadlines with consequences too dire for Mind to bear. He relented and I ascended, figuratively speaking, into the realm of inspired writing.

And Notre-Dame, this mighty cathedral, was the catalyst!

You're kidding! Look at this place. Gothic. Monstrous. Consumed by its own gravity. All stone and no life.

So how did you woo Inspiration?

No wooing required. She succumbed. Who wouldn't? Paris by night, glowing lights, pealing bells, the specter of Quasimodo working the bell ropes and leaping among the rafters. It all came together. The comet and the cathedral. The old girl was practically dancing.

And out of this comes Weasel, Dwarf and electricity bills?

And more! Care to hear my paean to psoriasis?

That would send CNN viewers straight to Fox. We're talking to Martin Raim, caught in the act, that rarest of phenomena, inspired writing. Walt Blizter, CNN.

I sit among the
posing friends, the
passing families, the
security guard named
Kami pausing for a
smoke break. Today,
the whole world
moves around
me.

Musée du Louvre
PARIS, FRANCE

Postcards

Your guiding force may be as near to you as the vein throbbing in your neck.

—Phil Cousineau, *Stoking the Creative Fires*

The Mirror of Love

Jean-Bernard Ponthus

INSIDE SHAKESPEARE AND Company Bookstore, a steep and narrow staircase with each step the size of a shoebox leads me to the upper floor, where antique books lie, not for sale but for display. The brown leather covers match the wooden staircase.

As I walk up, I notice a red velvet sofa up against a wall; this wall is covered with pieces of paper. In the interstice, I can just make out my reflection in what remains of a mirror. Some ID pictures are tacked up there. Are these people missing? I stare at scraps of paper, many-colored notes above my head.

Is this the wall of lamentation or adoration?

What are all the scriptures saying?

Sept. 14th, I'd love to come back to your city, Kyung-Soon from Seoul.

For all of us who shared this year in Paris, Sofia from Madrid.

Good vibrations.

Books are magic.

My favorite place.

On a previous visit, I remember, the mirror was clearly visible. A sentence in white paint was written on it: "The Mirror of Love." I had stared at myself then, wondering what that meant.

Now the mirror is saturated with prayers few could decipher, and as I turn the corner at the top of the shoebox stairs, I can no longer see my reflection.

All I see, like linen hanging on a rope above the sky, is love.

Water, Water

Ann Dufaux

THE OTHER DAY IN A SHOP in the Latin Quarter, I noticed an old postcard, a sepia picture of an apartment building on rue de Seine where my great-grandmother was once a concierge. What made the scene so dark and gloomy? Was it the mist rising up from the water, or the swirling soot descending from the chimney tops, or a combination of both? The dark buildings loomed along the street through the shadow. Had the photo been taken at dawn or dusk, or on an overcast day? The street looked like a Venetian canal, with four men in rowboats, moving along with poles. It had to be the 1910 flood. I turned the card over and I saw I was right.

Earlier this year, my friend Pierre and I sat in Café Boul' Mich' near the window, watching people rush for cover in the pouring spring rain, some clutching their umbrellas, others caught unawares and drenched to the bone. The wind was blowing and the rain lashed at the window pane. Pierre said, "Paris has major floods once every century. With the wet winter we've had plus global warming, the next one may be just 'round the corner."

An elderly gentleman at the table next to us said, "Parisians use the Zouave pillar upholding the Alma Bridge as a meter stick when the Seine overflows at the end of winter. It is a statue of a Zouave, a colonial soldier who wore a fez instead of a helmet. Paris never saw a year like 1910. The water went right up to his shoulders. Streets turned into rivers, sometimes a meter deep."

I often walk by that building on rue de Seine in which my great-grandmother, Adeline Rivière, gave birth to my Grandma Juliette at the height of the great flood, in early February 1910.

When I was a girl, whenever my parents came home late, Grandma Juliette would get me ready for bed. I remember one night when I was nine years old.

"I have a very special story to tell you tonight, something that really happened to our family."

She knew I preferred stories about my ancestors to *The Three Bears* or *Jack and the Beanstalk.*

She tucked me into bed and stretched out next to me. I leaned into her and my cheek sank into the soft knit of her sweater. I breathed in her familiar lavender scent.

"Tell me about your mama, Grandma."

"Your great-grandma Adeline was a hard-working woman, sweeping or scrubbing the hallway and the seven-story staircase from dawn to dusk. My father, Albert, was a mechanic who worked for the métro network. She had to feed him and mend, iron, and wash his clothes. Every week, she carried a heavy load of dirty linen to the local wash house. She spent half the day down on her knees, washing, rinsing, and wringing. In those days there were no washing machines, refrigerators, or electric irons, so she was out and about, even when she was pregnant with me."

"It had snowed a lot in northern France that year. The snow melted and it rained and rained. The rivers started rising and the Seine flooded many of our streets. One day, when my mother was pregnant with me, water started seeping under their front door. After two days the water was so deep that the kitchen stools and dining room chairs started floating around. Can you imagine? They couldn't stay in their lodgings on the ground floor. They had to move out. Luckily, their friends from the third floor, Mr. and Mrs. Bernard, offered to put them up.

Many families moved out of the city altogether. It was too difficult to get around and find food. Hardly anybody could get to work. You couldn't even see the steps leading down to the métro station! The black waters swept along, swirling down toward the platforms like a thundering waterfall. Nobody dared venture near the dark entrances for fear of being dragged deep down."

"What about Great-Grandpa and Great-Grandma?"

"For almost two months they were stuck in their building. Fortunately, volunteers went around the city by boat delivering dry beans, potatoes, bacon, bread, and gallons of clean water."

"What then?"

"I was due in early March at the nearby maternity. My mother was exceptionally modern for her day and believed that it was a lot safer to have babies in a hospital. One night, in early February she started having contractions—four weeks early. My father rushed to the window and, seeing no sign of any boats, turned ghostly pale. As he paced up and down he moaned, 'How on earth will we ever manage?' His wife calmly told him, 'Albert dear, go upstairs and knock on Miss Lucy's door. She's a nurse in training; she can help us.'"

I snuggled closer. "And you were born that night?"

"Yes, Miss Lucy turned out to be a very good midwife, and I was a healthy, strapping baby."

"But you told me that lots of big, frightened rats came up from the flooded métro tunnels and the cellars and swam along the streets trying to get away. Don't rat bites make people very sick?"

"They can, but those creatures were fearful and everybody in our building had cats, so the rats kept away."

"When did things get back to normal?"

"By the end of March. But when my parents went back with me to their apartment, their furniture was ruined. The sofa and mattresses were soaking wet. There was silt and mud all over the floor, the paint was peeling off the walls, and their linen was green with mold. Imagine how foul the smell was. The food left in the kitchen had gone rotten, and the mold growing on the damp wallpaper and wet upholstery gave off a disgusting mushroom-like odor. It took a long time and much cleaning, disinfecting, scrimping and saving before they were able to live in their home as comfortably as before."

"You said that Great-Grandma Adeline died young."

"That's right, darling, she died of tuberculosis, probably due to all that humidity."

———

Pierre pats me on the shoulder and asks me if I am all right. I feel pulled back from the past, where I had felt the sensations of my ancestors: the panic of my great-grandfather as he stood open-mouthed, staring at the waterfall on the steps of the métro station, and the fright of my stranded great-grandmother as she experienced the first pains of labor four weeks early.

I nod as I notice the rain has slowed and is now gently pattering on the café window. A pale sun shines down upon Paris through a break in the clouds.

Looking at People Looking at the *Mona Lisa*

Emily Seftel

AT THE LOUVRE, ONCE inside the Salle des États, you could be forgiven for cursing Leonardo da Vinci's choice of canvases. His masterpiece is only thirty by twenty-one inches, not nearly large enough to be visible through the wall of visitors milling in front of it, jockeying for an unobstructed view. It is mid-afternoon; the room is heaving with people here to pay homage to the *Mona Lisa,* or at least to her status. And you are part of this crowd, jostling for position, ignoring the other paintings in the room, trying to get a glimpse of the most famous smile in the world.

But for the moment you have no way of seeing it. You're only five-foot-three, and though you crane your head and stand on tiptoe, taller visitors crowd in front of you, broad backs and big hair obscuring the view. You risk an undignified jump or two to confirm the painting's presence, stopping when you inadvertently rake the instep of the person behind you. You make out the case surrounding the painting, camera flashes reflecting off the glass. Finally, you draw back and wait for a path to open.

The painting is now hidden by dozens of other tourists, mostly Chinese, although a group of Italians have managed to force their way through the scrum. Dark-haired heads bob in front of you; the instant one leaves, another pops up to take its place. You're reminded of the Whac-A-Mole game at the state fair, and stifle a brief urge to start bopping heads. Around you, hands shoot into the air, digital cameras thrust forward, human periscopes veering this way and that as they try to center the painting in their viewfinders. Small beads of sweat dot your hairline as still more people crowd into the room, and an uninterrupted stream of noise swirls around you: parents barking at their children, couples squabbling, guides shouting information to groups that only half-listen as they angle their cameras.

People come and go in a constant flow, like salmon fighting their way upstream, propelled more by impulse than by anything else. Pointing themselves in the direction of the *Mona Lisa,* they spare a few seconds to glance at her face before fumbling with the camera, waiting a bit longer to try to snap a photo with no other heads in it. A misleading photo, one that implies that its taker has worshiped alone at the altar of *La Joconde*, instead of throwing elbows at a group of Brazilian teenagers in order to maintain position.

For most people, the point of seeing the *Mona Lisa* is not, in fact, seeing the *Mona Lisa*. You've seen the face a million times

—on postcards, T-shirts, coasters. The point is to brag back home. "Yes, of course we saw the *Mona Lisa*. And you really can't tell if she's smiling. Hold on, I have a picture somewhere."

Finally the Chinese tourists leave, and you take advantage of the lull to move forward, camera ready. Before stowing your camera, you pause to confirm the successful completion of your mission. The viewing screen is filled with the *Mona Lisa* and her enigmatic smile. No other heads are visible. You have indeed worshipped alone.

Then you hurry out. It's a big museum, and you need to make sure you have time to get a picture of the *Venus de Milo*.

Visions

The author of the great myths and legends
is inside you.
And I don't mean that figuratively,
I mean it literally.
The intelligence and wisdom
that created those old, great stories
is inside you.

—James Bonnet, *Stealing Fire*
From the Gods

The End of August

Jane Weston

LIGHT STREAMS INTO THE station. Trains pull in, trains pull out, dirty and battered, shuddering with life. Noise reverberates up to the high, arched ceiling, as families, backpackers and professionals jostle. The departure board blinks, shuffling destinations and platforms. Espresso cups are hastily emptied, and cigarette smoke lingers. The season is turning, Parisians are returning from the south and the sea.

New beginnings infuse the air.

I step out from the double doors of a TGV marked MARSEILLE SAINT CHARLES—PARIS GARE DU LYON. My clothes are crumpled, but I'm dutifully blending in with the perennial Parisian insistence on darker fabrics. I would need to speak in my off-key French to be noticed as an Englishwoman. Now that I am out of the train, there are hollow pangs of absence in my chest.

I recently lost my mother in a brutal way. Since then, it's been hard to follow even simple conversations. I don't want a wave of grief to swell up in the midst of so many anonymous faces, so I push myself to concentrate, placing one foot in front of the other. As I near the exit, I lurch to avoid a toddler who has flopped to the floor. He falters between wailing and laughter as his mother lifts him to his feet.

Outside the station, buses rumble past with their packed cargo, jolting and bolting in tempo with the traffic lights. Drivers drum their fingers. The leaden humidity of the summer has lifted, and the city is picking itself up after a dormant August of boarded-up businesses. A few autumn leaves have already fallen, and cooler September air is testing its teeth. By the road, a man with a battered sports bag at his feet is shouting and jabbing his fists. Passersby give him a wide berth, stare through him, wary, weary. Sandwich stalls line the street in a cloud of melted cheese and fried meat. There are half-empty bars and generic supermarkets with stacks of plastic-wrapped fruits. They crowd into a space that only reluctantly gives way to the Paris of postcards.

The boulevard widens as I reach the Seine. Barges crawling along the river spark memories of my mother's visit one May. I watched from the sidewalk above. She stood on the quai, serene in her blue coat as she queued in the shade of Notre-Dame to board the Batobus. As the crowds began to hide her from view, she'd turned around to wave goodbye, calling out, "Good luck with your writing!"

As this memory surfaces, a sense of presence descends to fill the hollow space in my chest to the brim, as vivid as the summer light of the south. I feel I am being held in an embrace. I look beyond the gray rooftops and up to the sky, before covering my face with my hands.

Suddenly real arms are around my shoulders, and I see a familiar set of dark brown eyes, filled with concern.

"*Ça va? Qu'est-ce qui t'arrive?*"

I take a slow, calm breath.

"I feel like my mother is here with me. And that she's at peace, and will always love me."

I begin to cry, but feel lighter for the first time in weeks. I take his arm.

"Let's go home."

Finding My Inner Toga

Jennifer Flueckiger

JEALOUS. I'M NOT PROUD, but that was the only word for it.

The Saturday writing group had published an anthology, and I was in the audience the night they read their work at the legendary Paris bookstore, Shakespeare and Company. I was in the Tuesday anthology-less writing group and tried to hide the festering green wound that was growing on the side of my head.

I deserved to be in that anthology. My stuff was as good as theirs . . . right? My only crime seemed to be a different workshop meeting day and a different instructor. It was not fair.

I bandaged my sore and started a new session with my Tuesday group. This was the session I was going to produce the masterpiece; this was the session for glory.

The instructor made the announcement: We were invited to submit pieces for consideration for an anthology. Instead of excitement, I felt the bandage and scab ripped off the wound.

I had to be in that anthology. I did a quick mental scan of my back catalog of literary gems that were waiting to be given the breath of ink. Which one would be best? Which one should I choose? Most important, which one would the editors choose?

I looked at the rest of the group and thought I recognized pale looks of panic as they mentally searched for their best work. Some were friends. Some I'd just met. All were competitors.

Our instructor explained submissions were to be developed from the previous week's exercise. I had missed the first class. I didn't understand the assignment. This was not going the way it was supposed to go. I felt tightness across my chest. I could not catch my breath.

She read an email of support she had received while struggling with the outline of her novel (wouldn't it be nice to have an idea for a novel?). It said something about writers having the gift of all of the great storytellers throughout time inside them.

Then I got a vision: the instructor floating on a cloud, dressed in white, quill in one hand. Cherubs—carrying beautiful, leather-bound books embossed with her name—flew between her and an adjacent cloud upon which stood Homer, Scheherazade, Shakespeare, the Brontës and Twain, all in togas, smiling broadly, giving her the big thumbs-up. My fellow writing-group members—also toga-ed up—were on a nearby cloud, waiting to receive their blessing from the literary gods. I was watching the whole scene from down on Earth though a broken telescope.

The blessed instructor then asked the blessed group members to work on their mystical, undoubtedly publishable pieces. They quickly brought out notebooks, pens, and computers. There was no trace of the previous panic or doubtful looks; pure inspiration illuminated their faces.

Oh God, I thought, this was my last chance to fly. I asked the instructor to explain the assignment to me once again. *Please don't speak in angel tongue*, I begged with my eyes. *This mortal needs to ascend to the clouds.* She said the previous week she had asked the group to go to different parts of Shakespeare and Company, look at the bookshelf, and write the first thing they were inspired to write before their internal censor took over.

"For instance, I might write about this," she said as she pulled a book from the shelf. "I've done research on this author."

Of course you have, I thought; and of course the author was utterly unknown to me.

"Or London," she said, and grabbed a book creatively titled *London.* "You could write about your experiences of being in London."

But I'm from Edinburgh, I thought.

"Literally pick anything here and write about what you instantly think about, what instantly inspires you."

Nothing. Nothing. Nothing. I will never be published. I stared at the wall of books in front of me. A yellow book called *Modern Studies* was the only title on which I could focus. Modern studies? Modern studies! What was I supposed to do with that? I had to do something. I looked back at the shelf in desperation for something else, anything else. All I could see were books that meant nothing to me or blurry titles.

Then a book fell from the top shelf and hit me on the head. Then another book, then a few more, and a few more, until all of the books on the ceiling-high shelf came cascading down, burying me under the weighty tradition of great storytellers whose work I didn't know enough about and of whose club I was not a member.

Dusty books all around me, an oozing green wound, and a throbbing, bruised ego.

I give up, I thought. I let out a long sigh and closed my eyes, hoping this would dull the pain.

When I opened them I saw, through the pile of books, a shaft of light highlighted by the settling dust. I followed it through the scattered spines and bent pages. It landed on my pen, which had been knocked on top of a green cloth-bound book in the middle of the pile.

Unable to move the rest of my body, I wrestled my arm free and grabbed my pen. I wrapped my fingers around it and knew what I had to do. I tightened my grip and punched through the top of the pile. My hand and pen were free.

"So it's really that simple," the instructor said.

"Thanks," I said. "I get it now." I walked back to my seat wondering how I might look in a toga.

Vermilion Cygnet

Sana Chebaro

BALLERINAS PAMPER themselves with powder and perfume in air filled with the acrid smell of sweat. A flaxen-haired girl stretches her lithe limbs on the bar, bending and pushing her muscular shoulders forward. A petite blonde holds on to her ankle and extends her hamstring against the wall. Lilia, the youngest ballerina, a button-nosed brunette, drifts among the hustle and bustle. She is just about fourteen.

Lilia finds an armchair, wipes some crumbs off the cushion, and wiggles herself into the seat.

She notices an ashen girl emerging from the bathroom. The girl cups a hand to her mouth, knocks her head back, and swallows hard. She takes a deep breath through her nostrils and exhales heavily, emptying her lungs, tensing her abdomen. She gently lifts her head, lengthening it upward, as if her crown were tied to the ceiling by a delicate thread. She opens her arms and fills her girth with air. Her lateral muscles expand; her chest is raised high, making her legs weightless. With her sculpted calves, she reaches a pointe pose, satisfied at the sound of her joints cracking.

Lilia watches as the girls flirt amongst each other with bare breasts, nude tights, wide smiles and delirious laughter. Their sparkling tutus bob up and down with each movement, floating around their narrow hips. Wine is poured high in dirty bistro glasses, gulped over costumes, trickling down chins. A ballerina rubs a lipstick-stained tooth with her forefinger as a friend tries to apply some color to her lips. A dancer combs her raven locks, coiling them into a spiraling bun at the stem of her neck, pulling them tight against her head, stretching out her eyes like a cat's. As Lilia's legs dangle, swinging playfully, her head darts from side to side as she observes two ballerinas in a tug-of-war over a dress. They lunge forward and lurch back until they are enshrouded in a cloud of tulle and organza. Last-minute fussing is made over lost headbands and slippers, the covering up of bruises and the mending of moth-eaten tights.

Lilia feels cold, rough fingers taking a firm grip on her arm. She looks up to see an old lady with white hair, a look of relief on her gaunt features. She leads Lilia away, placing her in the care of a freckled, red-headed dancer who gleams with excitement, wrapping her arm around the young ballerina like a giant swan coddling her cygnet. She finds a quiet corner in which to attend to Lilia's preparations while the bevy follows, flocking and cooing around her. They pull and twist her hair into a French plait as she grimaces with discomfort. They envelope her blistered feet in gauze and wrap pink ribbons around her ankles.

Lilia wets and bites her lower lip in anticipation, knowing it is almost show-time. The redhead startles her, swooping down to plant a bright red kiss on her cheek. She grabs Lilia's hand and leads her to the support troupe while the young ballerina furiously rubs her cheek with the back of her hand.

Lilia holds her breath behind the velvet curtain.

She closes her eyes, drowning out the frenzy backstage.

The orchestra begins its tender refrain.

She takes a deep breath, her lungs heaving under her corset.

The curtain parts and she breezes onto the stage. Her arms float with the soft melody of the harp. Her gaze is melancholic. Her slippers sweep the floor with the sighs of violins and she tiptoes to the piano's high notes, pausing into an arabesque.

The cellos tremble with present danger. Her eyes become fretful. The high-pitched flute chimes with the fluttering of her feet. As the trumpets build on the rhythmic fervor, the quivering of her slippers becomes ever more frantic.

There is a rustle of keys, and a horn bellows across the stage. There is panic as dancers rush to assume position. Edgar Degas walks in from the biting cold, props his hat and coat on an old oak hanger, and rubs his icy hands together. He sits on a stool, admiring his latest creation, the figures frozen in ethereal poses. He chuckles to himself, and with his little finger ever so surgically wipes a bright vermilion spot from the youngest ballerina's cheek. He takes a step back to scrutinize her details, her precise, outstretched leg and regal shoulders.

He beams with satisfaction, bewitched by her defiant air.

Memory

You can't get to any of these truths by sitting in a field
smiling beatifically, avoiding your anger and damage and grief.
We don't have much truth to express unless
we have gone into
those rooms and closets and abysses
we were told not to go into.

—Anne Lamott, *Bird by Bird*

Dinner
Laura Mandel

Like all rituals, this one brings her comfort. It's easy and rehearsed, thoughtless, like waking up each day, turning on her side to face her husband and saying, "Good morning, dear." This ritual involves opening the door to the dining room, propping it open with a wedged plastic door stop, and laying two place mats on the table, at precisely 6:30 p.m.. The room, so still it is almost stale, always smells faintly of old wood, perhaps the lingering scent of the large oak table. The only sound is the slow shuffling of her feet against the sand-colored carpet, the light rattling of the china inside the antique cabinets. It's another mundane evening.

Returning to the kitchen, she stands in front of the sink and looks out of the small window overlooking the backyard, framed by stained white lace curtains. Her lips turn up softly as she thinks about the thousands of times she has stood in this very spot. As she watched her children play through the window, time would stop.

She washes a few pieces of lettuce and peels some carrots for a salad, then goes downstairs to fetch frozen chicken breasts from the basement freezer. Carrying them up the steep, dark staircase, she feels the sting of ice against her hands. She brings up some rugelach, too. It's been frozen since Barbara and the grandkids came over for lunch last month.

Two place mats, two plates, two glasses, two forks and two knives. (Has it really been thirty years since there were four place mats, four plates?) A pitcher of iced tea in the center of the table. The faint noise of the TV from the bedroom—evening news on high volume—permeates the walls to enter the kitchen and mingle with the rich smell of roasting chicken, of herbs and butter and tender meat.

"Allan," she says, "it's time for dinner."

She watches him as he eats, as she herself takes only small, occasional bites ("You've gotten too thin," he says.) She thinks about how lucky he is to still eat with such pleasure and ease, while she has grown gaunt with age, having lost the appetite of her youth. As he cleans his plate, he thanks her with a small, turned-up, toothy smile, saying (without saying), *I love you the way I've loved you for sixty years.* Then he asks for a glass of vodka on ice and returns to the bedroom, to the TV.

She clears the table, folds the place mats and places them in the cupboard drawer, closes the dining room door behind her. She reflects on tomorrow evening's meal. Roast beef sandwiches or brisket? Green beans or barley? She can bake a sour-cream coffee cake, or buy that chocolate loaf from the store and top it with some vanilla ice cream and canned cherries.

She thinks to herself that there is nothing new under the sun, which is good, because Allan likes it that way.

Standing over the sink again, looking out over the yard where blackberries grew, where she once saw a family of wild turkeys grazing on the daffodils ("Are the turkeys back today?" the grandkids would ask every Thanksgiving) she begins to wipe the plates with a dishcloth, suds from the soap covering her wrinkled hands, and stack them on the counter to dry. She remembers how the kids used to play in the wintertime, chasing one another up the snow-covered hill on the far end of the yard, all the way to the top, until they were out of sight, then running back down again, piercing the cold air with their delighted shrieks, their brown hair flapping behind them in the wind.

She scrapes at the burned oil on the blackened skillet. She runs the sponge around the edges of the rusted hot plates on the stove. She imagines that the kids are asleep in their beds, that Barbara is four and that Dickie is eight and that there is no rust on the stove top. Gently closing her eyes, she feels the blood rush through her veins, from her tired eyelids all the way to the tips of her gnarled fingers.

She feels a sharp, sudden pain in her chest.

It is a chilly day in March and the kids are starting to arrive. They head straight to the kitchen. Their father had called the day before to tell them the news. "She was on the floor by the dishwasher," he said. "It must have happened after dinner."

They begin to clear out the cabinets and cupboards, to make piles of plates and bowls, of small white ceramic ramekins, of steak knives and espresso cups. Barbara tucks the old-fashioned lemon juicer into her purse. She packs up sets of Ginori china dinnerware for her two daughters. ("You might want them when you buy your first apartments," she tells them.) Cardboard boxes line the walls; stacks of glass, ceramic, and wrought iron cover the yellow-tiled floor. The kitchen is full, and empty.

Dick comes up from the basement with a bottle of expired supermarket wine and a Tupperware full of frozen rugelach. Holding it with both hands, feeling its frozen sting against his skin, he focuses on each steep, narrow step. He thinks of his mother and her daily dinnertime commute down to the basement, and then, the smell of her chicken.

Free to Breathe

Leslie Lemons

NEIGHBORHOODS MUSHROOMED overnight in the pastureland surrounding Dallas, Texas in the years following World War II. Friendships were forged as fathers debated the best grass seed, mothers exchanged favorite recipes, and kids played hopscotch on the sidewalk. Our family landed in Lake Highlands when I was four years old.

Susan lived across the street and our games were never-ending. We built tents out of card tables and blankets, played at mothering our dolls, and plotted about how to sneak into Ali Baba's cave to steal his treasure. When we grew older we chased the boys next door and practiced our baton twirling in the backyard. On summer evenings we'd beg to stay outside just ten more minutes to sprawl on the lawn and watch for falling stars. When it was time for lights out, I would flip the switch on my flashlight to signal a final good night, and a beam would answer from across the street.

I was nine when my mother sat me down and announced, "We're moving to a new town in a new state, New Mexico, with mountains nearby where we'll build a cabin and spend our summers." She paused and, with no response from me, said, "Now, isn't this going to be an exciting adventure?"

I let myself get swept along in my mother's plans and fantasized about being a cowgirl "way out West." Susan and I were Annie Oakley fans, and often dressed up in matching leather-fringed skirts and ruby red cowboy boots and hats to watch the weekly adventure series. I imagined myself performing acrobatic tricks on the back of a palomino horse with my fringed skirt flying and a cowboy hat flung back from a string around my neck.

But at times I felt overwhelmed and uneasy. My mother's enthusiastic energy seemed a ploy to distract me from dwelling on why this might not be the best thing since sliced bread.

I climbed into our loaded Chevy and leaned out the window to wave goodbye to Susan, who stood on her front porch clutching her mother's hand and biting her lip. I jumped out of the car and ran to her. I breathed in her scent and realized that I might never see her again. I ran to the car without looking back, slumped down in the back seat, tears streaming down my cheeks, and pulled my knees to my chest, hiding my face between my knees.

We arrived in Carlsbad, New Mexico, in late November to frigid cold and blinding snowstorms, the worst weather in recorded history. I was an outsider at school, shy and embarrassed to reach out, and avoided even my parents. I hid in my bedroom every night, doing my homework, staring absent-mindedly out the curtain-less window, listening to the wind and snow spit against the thin glass of the windowpane.

One night in January I woke up gasping for air. I sucked in what I could and fell into a troubled sleep. After that I often awoke in a struggle to catch my breath, and began to have visions of a midnight strangler.

Several weeks later, I was ripped from sleep with my throat completely constricted, unable to breathe. I was sure I was choking to death, and my heart raced. I thrashed in the sheets, and the bed thumped against the wall loudly enough to wake my mother, who placed a warm cloth upon my forehead and whispered until I fell asleep.

My mother had me tested for asthma, and we learned I was allergic to dust.

When summer arrived, it brought a dry, intense heat that left me listless and bored. We were stuck in Carlsbad because the mountain cabin was not yet finished. In my mind, there were only two things of beauty in that town: the Pecos River, where I dangled my toes in the cool water and imagined river-tubing down the lazy current to Texas and Susan, and the public library, a mysterious adobe pueblo hidden among ancient pecan trees, home to Indians in the old times.

Mother signed me up for the library's reading program. The first time I visited, the gnarled trees towered over me, the foliage so dense the sunshine sparkled like scattered diamonds among the leaves. As I opened the carved wooden door, a swoosh of cool air greeted me. The peace and quiet and intoxicating scent of books, leather, and wood filled me with anticipation of what I might discover among the thousands of volumes.

I often rode my bike to the adobe library to read in one of the leather chairs or outside under a canopy of green. At night, I would flip the switch on my flashlight and read under the sheet into the wee hours of the morning. I devoured *Anne of Green Gables, The Little Princess* and *Black Beauty.*

Little Women, set during the Civil War, drew me in. I admired impetuous, rebellious Jo, who gave up love and wealth to become a writer, and felt protective of Beth, who accepted her own frailty and gave her energy to others.

One late afternoon, as I read curled up under my favorite tree, where the branches, laced with light, enfolded me in a soft glow, I realized Beth was dying. She and Jo were on the beach, soaking in the sun, with Beth resting her head on Jo's lap. I closed my eyes, afraid to continue. My chest began to ache and my throat tightened; I remembered Susan on her front porch, wiping her eyes and leaning against her mother, waving goodbye. As I read "the bitter wave of their great sorrow broke over them," I hunched over as tears spilled onto the page.

A falling leaf brushed against my wet cheek, bringing me back to earth, and I squinted into the setting sun, closed the book and hugged it to my chest. The hot, heavy air suddenly seemed lighter and cooler, and I felt free to breathe.

Seu Juca

Maria Bitarello

"WILL YOU COME BACK?" Seu Juca asks in a trembling voice on our second visit.

I look at him, his arms searching for something or someone to lean on as we go over a step and into the kitchen together, all of us—family and film crew. His eyes match the pleading in his voice.

"Yes, of course, we're coming back—on Friday, as we discussed before," I whisper, lending him my arm for balance. "We can have you sign these papers then."

I nod to the sheet of paper I have under the arm I'm using to help him sit down by the kitchen table. He lets go of me to sit down, folds both of his hands, and rests them on his lap. He doesn't talk. Not today.

Seu Juca lives in a simple house that he built from scratch. He has a family to call his own—wife, kids, in-laws, grandchildren—all of whom stand beside, behind and around him in the kitchen.

"And you'll come back, right?"

"Yes. On Friday."

He stares at me in silence.

"Would Saturday be a good day? Better?" he asks.

He meant were we coming back after we finished shooting the interview for the documentary film we were making.

"Yes," I reply. "Yes."

His age is unknown to us, but Seu Juca is an elderly man whose left leg is nine centimeters shorter than his right. He doesn't limp properly, but swaggers, much like a pirate. His walk is accompanied by a steady yet vague stare some feet ahead of him, down toward the ground. He shows only minor difficulty getting about his small house, moving slowly when he goes up stairs or sits down. Outside, he uses a broomstick to shake the branches of a lemon tree in his front yard, but lets the kids pick up the lemons and bring them inside to the kitchen.

On our third visit, he tells his story.

"I was coming into the plant and a bunch of them guys were protesting and blocking the entry. I was young," he tells us as we assemble in his kitchen. "I was young, but I had nothing to do with the quarrels that started the night before. That morning, on the seventh, I was there. And I got hit."

He stares straight into the camera without hesitation, and with a hand gesture indicates his left leg.

On October 7, 1963, the workers of a giant steel factory in Ipatinga, Brazil, and the army enacted what came to be known as the Massacre of Ipatinga.

"All it took was some fool to throw a rock at them tanks and they started shooting at us. I still got the bullet in my leg."

The fragments spread between his shin and thigh. He went back to work a few months later, but once his contract ended, he was laid off. Over the years, the steelworkers' union had tried to contact Seu Juca. They saw political leverage in his case, but Seu Juca wanted no part in it; he knew they didn't really care about him. During the filming of the documentary, the union even tried to use us to get close to him, but we refused.

"No one stopped by to see how we were doing. No help was ever offered." When we come back to film his interview the following day, the kitchen is bright. Discreet yet visible, a thin layer of opaque moisture covers his eyes, but no tears.

"I won't sign nothing."

He turns around, toward the garage. He raised his family, built his house and lived his life on a state pension.

"Do you understand why we need your signature?"

"What are you going to do with it?"

"Keep it. It stays with us. It is permission to film you."

The next day, I come back alone. Seu Juca agrees to sign the papers. He reaches for my hand. Warm and dry, his hands feel rough in mine while our fingers search for a grip. I know I can't undo the wrong that was done to this man; he knows it, too. But we both feel respect and trust in that grip.

We finish filming, and though I remember his request to return, we are busy editing the film and soon leave the country.

—·∞∞·—

Fourteen months later, Seu Juca died. We did not hear about it until a year later when we received the news by email, gathered around the computer. As the words were read out loud, my thoughts drifted to the memory of Seu Juca's face as he asked us to return, and the feel of his hand squeezing mine. His silence had become mine.

He never watched our film.

Not long before he died, he was given a small sum of money by the government to amend the situation, half a century after he was shot. Not nearly what was rightfully his, but a settlement nonetheless, and a sense of closure, I suppose. He used the money to take his wife, Ritelina, to Portugal, where their oldest son lives. Ritelina passed away shortly after their return home, and Seu Juca followed two weeks later.

I remembered a close-up of his face in the film, saying, "For a long time, no one opened their mouths."

I thought of the memorial near a shopping mall in Ipatinga. It sits in the middle of the intersection of a busy avenue, inaccessible to pedestrians, with nowhere to cross or to park. No more than a landmark, perhaps, to help locate the mall. We took Seu Juca there once, but with his bad leg, he could never make it across the avenue to receive something solid in recognition of his injuries.

"And now, still we hear nothing . . . it's been forgotten."

We shot *Silêncio 63* in 2009, and it is now 2011. We made the film to show the injustice of the massacre to the world, to prevent people from forgetting. There's a signed contract in a folder at home and, as promised, we're keeping it.

But we never went back to see him.

Birds call, spring winds
blow, cottonball clouds move across
the cerulean sky. Four students
huddle together on the steps,
swigging champagne straight
from the bottle.
This is Paris.

Basilica de Sacré Cœur
MONTMARTRE, PARIS.

Mystery

Mystery is a resource, like coal or gold, and its preservation is a fine thing.

—Tim Cahill, writer

Wrapped

Catalina Girón

LIKE A LEAD SOLDIER AND a ballerina doll, they stood next to each other.

There was no expression on their faces.

He was wearing a black suit, but he kept it casual: no tie. She had a red silk dress with white dots, blue high heels, and a headband in her hair.

They stood a long step apart, their faces and bodies facing the métro at Passy's open-air station. He didn't look at her, nor she at him.

An autumn breeze approached, making her skirt dance, lifting her long black hair, which lightly caressed his face. He took a deep breath, hoping to capture her scent.

A little girl was laughing, holding tight to a tattered rabbit toy. She ran in circles around them while her smiling father chased her, wrapping the silent couple in a space apart from the rest of the world.

More people arrived, reducing the space between them. Their faces were unperturbed, still facing the same direction. His trembling fingers betrayed his nervousness.

He took one small step to the side, coming closer to her, and still looking ahead, slowly raised his hand until it brushed her dancing dress. The breeze stopped. He touched her fingertips. She carefully slipped her hand into his and raised her chin toward a ray of sunlight that shone a triangular shape on her skin.

Holding hands, the ballerina doll and the lead soldier held their breath, willing this second to last forever, until the rumble of an incoming train interrupted their silence. He smiled and she blushed. It started to rain.

It was a good start for a very first date.

The Paved Streets of Paris

Claire Fallou

THE ELEGANT STREETS, breezy boulevards and winding alleys of our beloved Paris were once paved with square pieces of stone. Most Parisians have seen their delicate patterns in old pictures, their endless geometry of arches, squares, and diamonds interwoven on the ground in certain preserved places; and older Parisians remember with nostalgia how they would shine at night under the street lamps, their flat tops glowing and cracks lost in darkness in a meandering mosaic of light and shadow.

I often imagine the time when Paris hummed with the cobblestone industry. Thousands of workers filled the air with the powdery smell of freshly ground granite. If you got close to the warehouses near the Seine, you could hear the symphony the stones created as the chisels of dust-covered carvers chipped them by the hundreds. The music would resonate throughout the city, floating above its swarming roofs, up to the leafy Montmartre hill where lovers would listen to that silvery flutelike melody as they kissed.

It was the masons' backbreaking task to lay the pavers on the streets in neatly staggered rows. Those faceless men spent their days kneeling in the dirt, their bodies sore from the weight of the granite, but in those days no one pitied a working man. Paris lived on around them, often adding to their pain by means of a kicking horse or foul waters splashed into the street by a busy matron with a rag tied around her head.

On the river the barges came and went, loaded with stones picked upstream in the Norman quarries. As was then the custom in fluvial freight, the captains in command were usually second-rate seamen fit only to amuse the master mariners of Brest or Marseille. What they lacked in technique, however, they made up for in colour. "ATTACH THOSE DAMN ROCKS, you filthy son of a pike!" they'd yell between two swigs of a rough Beaujolais. Then they'd wipe their mouths with the back of their sleeves and burst out laughing, and their great laughs would echo down the river to a crossing barge, whose captain would blow a horn as a traditional greeting. If you have ever met a boisterous captain anywhere in the world, he may have had Norman ancestors on the Seine.

Yes, it was all well organized; yet there were major downsides to this efficient industry. The pavers were Paris's weakest point. Whenever one stone was picked off its bed, it could cause mayhem.

The Revolution started exactly this way in 1789, when a member of the tax-laden Third Estate fired a paver at the Bastille. As a squadron of royal guards passed by in formation, an unidentified blacksmith dropped his tools, bent over, grabbed a loose block, and threw it vigorously. The stone flew straight to the walls of the prison where it landed with a loud thump.

The subsequent Three Glorious Days of 1830, as well as the numerous outbreaks thereafter, dutifully perpetuated the tradition; whenever one king's rule was felt too heavily someone always came forth, a thick man in brownish trousers or a formidable woman with a dirty apron, to uproot the first revolutionary stone and hurl it across the sky as a call to arms. The last of it happened in May 1968, when long-haired students in bell-bottom trousers levered the blocks off with iron sticks to fling them at the police.

Even under well-liked governments the cobblestones meant trouble. The legend remains of a certain Comte de Rocquen-court, friend to the archbishop and highly regarded in court, who once tripped over a misplaced block and fell face down in the gutter. A lowly baronet driving by in a gilded *calèche* had the nerve to laugh; a duel ensued and the comte, not so skilled with a sword as with social connections, ended up lying on the pavement for good. In 1959 Simone de Beauvoir, walking to the Café de Flore to meet Sartre, caught her heel in a crack; her shoe broke with a fearful sound, leaving its heel helplessly stuck in the ground, and Paris's reputation for both feminine charm and intellect swiftly shattered.

The blocks had become Fortune's devilish instrument.

That is why such a beautiful urban feature, designed in the old days to enhance the splendor of the City of Lights, in the end seemed only to serve the purpose of destruction. The pavers had to go. In the seventies, I imagine a mayor with a great mustache and a severe black suit ordering them to be dug up, and solid asphalt layered in their place on the Parisian ground.

For weeks the city was lost in a fog of dust. Vehicles were grounded at home. Dogs pulled their paws out of black, pungent tar. People tried to protest, but the stock of pavers was closely monitored.

To this day, it remains a mystery where all the stones went.

Some say they will reappear when the time has come for another revolution. I think they're gone for good. Just like the mighty monuments you see everywhere in Paris—the Louvre, the Conciergerie, the Châtelet—they belong to a roaring time we have silenced forever.

In some restored places you can still get a chance to see them, but they are glued in solid mortar so that they'll safely remain where they are supposed to. At the foot of Notre-Dame the stones no longer huddle together by their own free will; someone has poured a sticky river of black slime in the cracks, separating them from one another and forever trapping them in dirt and silent anonymity.

I imagine the roar, and wish.

The Chair

Kate Buljanovic

ANA LOOKED AROUND the shoebox apartment. Out of the corner of her eye, she saw a mouse scurry across the floor and disappear into a corner. Two weeks earlier she had moved from South Africa to Paris for a man she loved, truly expecting perfection.

That morning she woke up to the sour taste of the previous night's shouting and sobbing. She realized that the man she now saw under the glaring spotlight of proximity was entirely different from the one she had loved from a distance.

At first, his will to impress her had itself impressed her: his slapstick dance routines that exposed two-toned pastel socks, or the way he would wake her up in the morning by tickling her nose. When he placed the palm of her hand in his, his touch had soothed her restlessness.

Now, after only two weeks, she tripped over his clothes, which were tossed like petals on the floor, listened with a scowl as he revealed daily plans made without consulting or including her, and squinted at him as he cut his toenails with one leg perched on the basin. These days when he rubbed her collarbone, she shuddered and slowly drifted out of his reach.

This morning he had informed her, with two days' notice, that they would spend the weekend in the South, together every second.

As she glanced around the apartment she remembered she knew no one except him in this city. Scenes of all she had left in South Africa ran through her mind: farewell parties with friends lifting glasses to her, and barefoot walks in the garden with the sun warming her face. She felt tears drop like pins onto her blouse as she grabbed her keys and left.

Stumbling through the crooked streets of Paris, Ana remembered sitting with her family around an African blackwood table covered in crisp Egyptian cotton, upon which sat porcelain plates and quartz crystal glasses. Her mother's diamond ring caught the light as she placed a bright bowl of salad on the table. Laughter echoed as Ana's Uncle Simon scratched his bald head and told stories of sailing and olive picking on the Adriatic coast.

Ana lodged her foot in an uneven step and lunged forward. The street was empty and she shouted, "What was I thinking, coming here? No family, no friends, no job, no life . . . and all because of *love*?" The last word echoed through the buildings.

She felt something soft brush her leg and looked down to see a ragged dog peering at her through one eye. Champagne-colored fur covered the other eye; the dog was a tall, shaggy creature who wagged his tail and barked as if to reassure her that the world was listening.

Ana continued until she came across a bookshop nestled in a cobbled alley. Like an oil painting it pulsed with color. The shop's wooden frame was painted in green and solar yellow, as if to shout the words of spring. Low whispers of people's voices and piano notes drifted down from an open window upstairs.

Ana felt a sense of familiarity at the sweet smell of fried doughnuts and the quiet humming of English words. Musicians perched in front of the store playing jazzy tunes. Behind them, ruffled books sat like a stack of colorful feathers on shelves set up outside. People stretched across the shabby artisan chairs as if they had been there for decades.

None of the chairs were well kept or manicured, but they exuded something human as they peered out from underneath bodies that chatted away or read quietly as they smoked the last puff of a cigarette. The chairs seemed to have a wisdom of their own, as if they had seen the lives of people and experienced some of their woes. Ana imagined that the chairs had tasted ice-cream drips, felt the pleasure of sweet words and the pain of grainy wounds, heard the sighs of violin strings and the ruffle of chiffon, and smelled strands of clean hair.

Ana noticed one chair that sat alone, off to one side. It seemed to be isolated from its companions, who were clustered together, draped with people's bodies. This chair's navy paint was cracked and discolored, worn down by people who had printed their skin, their clothes, and their belongings upon its lap.

Ana felt drawn to it, and an ache in her feet pushed between her toes as she moved toward it. She freed her bag's leather straps from her chest and sank into the tattered chair, which seemed to extend its arms and wrap itself around her. She leaned her shoulders against its curve and felt her limbs loosen.

Ana closed her eyes, brushed a wisp of hair away from her forehead, and breathed the sweetness of the sugary air to shut out the world around her.

Perfection, she thought to herself, is nothing but a mere fallacy of the mind.

Energy rushed to her fingertips, tingling like warm mint. Ana slowly opened her eyes and looked around. She thought to herself that perhaps the city was not hers, not yet, but she had found this one place.

She burrowed more deeply into the chair.

Duende

The duende, then, is a power, not a work.
It is a struggle, not a thought.
Every man and every artist,
whether he is Nietzsche or Cézanne,
climbs each step in the ladder of his perfection
by fighting his duende,
not his angel, as has been said, nor his muse.

—Federico García Lorca, *In Search of Duende*

If in These Eyes

Laura Orsal

A MONTH AFTER THE baby died, Emma walked into the old bookstore, where the white-bearded bookseller was like a character in an old black-and-white American movie: Perched on a stool and immersed in a book, he looked up over his rounded glasses whenever a customer came in. Several ladders leaned against the shelves to let the most word-hungry readers reach the books up high.

Emma noticed the words *Live for humanity* written in white on a red-painted step to the left of the cash desk. Surrounded by the philosophy section and the poetry section, *Live for humanity* seemed right at home. In the tightly crowded corner that was the poetry section, Emma came across a collection by Lord Byron which she opened to a random page. She whispered the first stanza of the poem *My Soul is Dark*:

"My soul is dark—Oh! Quickly string
The harp I yet can brook to hear;
And let thy gentle fingers fling
Its melting murmurs o'er mine ear.
If in this heart a hope be dear,
That sound shall charm it forth again
If in these eyes there lurk a tear,
'Twill flow, and cease to burn my brain."

She remembered the moment in the hospital room as she waited for the baby to take his first breath. She had stared at his closed eyelids, willing them to open. She had heard the midwife announce his death and watched the woman carry him across the room and out the door.

In the bookstore, she walked to the shelves against the back wall, where there were more than twenty novels by Ernest Hemingway. *A Farewell to Arms, The Sun Also Rises* . . . this author had created stories out of his troubled mind. She wondered if each story had torn away at his heart, until one day he had woken up to find it gone.

At the very end of the library, Emma discovered a small hidden room, its entrance blocked off by iron bars, through which she could see rows upon rows of faded and dusty books filling the shelves and covering the floor. She wanted to walk right through those iron bars into that room, and remove herself from the real world by sitting on a pile of books, plunging into her favorite characters' lives, and forgetting her own.

She turned and walked up a narrow staircase, each step creaking. On the wall facing the banister, a drawing of the gaunt face of Oscar Wilde stared at her. She thought of Wilde's imprisonment, exile, and illness.

Once upstairs, she saw a mirror covered with little pieces of scrap paper, notes from tourists and readers from all around the world. She read: *I am very happy to have discovered this place. S.*

Emma walked along the narrow corridor, passing by a large, maze-like room filled with books, sofas, a bed, and a piano on which a young man was playing a melancholic tune. His fingers lightly touched the keys, and his hands swept from side to side. The music warmed her, and she felt lulled as the notes led her forward into a tiny, Victorian-style sitting room where people sat reading or gazing at the shelves.

Emma sat down and leaned back. She winced and clutched her middle as pain that pierced like needles moved from her womb up into her stomach. A black-and-white photograph of Walt Whitman met her eyes. Under a felt hat, one eyebrow was raised over eyes that seemed to see her. His mouth, buried in a white beard, curved in a small smile.

She closed her eyes and listened to people chatting and the hum of traffic passing by through the open window. Inside, she felt a few of the needles loosen and dissolve.

A cold draft came into the room and danced around her. She shivered.

Escape

Based on the photo *Porte d'Aubervilliers, 1932* by Henri Cartier-Bresson

Erin Byrne

THE BOY WAS THE POOREST of the poor in Paris between wars. He stopped and his feet slid inside worn shoes, which sank with an ooze in the mud. Underneath a grimace of gray sky, he leaned against the tin wall of the hovel he called home and listened to the chaos within.

Scraping, clawing, scuffling. Yelling, screaming, crying. Bumping, knocking, thumping. The last vestige of hope drained from his body; soon his father would come for him. The cold metal clawed his shoulder through an overcoat that weighed down his frame.

Panic spread from his stomach in escalating surges, poisonous petals growing with each pulsating push to grip and twist his bowels. His lungs were afraid to admit air.

He sought escape from the maelstrom with every vibrating atom of his being. He waited. And waited.

He reached out his empty little soul. His face took on a concentrated intensity. His eyes focused, unfocused. His chest slowed its rhythms, his mouth fell slack. His hearing slowly muffled, the violence became silence. The cold metal released his shoulder, and gloom gave up its quest to permeate. His dirt-caked body felt clean—and then he left it behind.

In this moment, though he did not know it, the boy instinctively practiced the ancient art of Transcendental Meditation.

Sunlight crept along the filthy slum, glinted on the window's jagged glass, and turned the mud a tawny tan. It moved as if seeking him. It snuck over the folds of the boy's soiled cap and rippled down his arm. Wave upon wave of warm, liquid love infused the center of his chest and rolled through his veins.

The sunlight was gentle, like a hand blessing him.

Life With Tobias

(excerpt from a longer work)

Philip Murray-Lawson

ALL DURING THE WAR, my mother had warned me, "If the Russians find out that you are the son of a war criminal, Christian, I dread to think what might happen."

When she died, she sent me to find her old friend Tobias, who lived in Lisoria, a port on the Danube. Tobias owed her a favor, she said.

I found Tobias's home, and he agreed to rent me some rooms. The house was filled with poor, broken denizens, two of whom, a one-armed woman named Klara who haunted the darkness of the stairs, and a mutilated soldier who squatted all day upon Tobias's doorstep, seemed to wish to communicate with me. Going to and from my rooms, I feared that even to brush them with my shoe would bring bad luck. If ever a blackened claw were thrust forth in hopes of a coin, I would avert my eyes, press on, and not slow until the street had been crossed. I allowed myself little curiosity about their presence; I had accepted them as easily as I had my dismal rooms.

I soon became friends with Tobias's daughter, Judith, and one day Tobias walked in on the two of us talking. He was furious. "Young man, when I agreed to rent you rooms, it was not an invitation to debauch my daughter."

It was 1945 and the war was over, but are wars ever over? Are they ever really won or lost?

The day after Tobias discovered me with Judith, I had to meet him to pay the rent. I knocked on the door with feelings of anger and trepidation. He was seated, as usual, at the wobbly table, fumbling with his scissors and some photographs.

"Keep away from Judith," he said. "She's suffered enough."

"I would prefer it if you knocked before entering my rooms," I began, referring to his unexpected entrance earlier. However, even as I spoke, my determination slipped away. I had slept but little and my head and bones ached. I wondered whether I was ill.

"You and Judith cannot be together," Tobias said. "The past cannot be erased. Listen to me. I understand these things. If you're not careful, your past will become your prison."

His meaning escaped me. He went on and on—as the old do—about how the past never dies, how it fashions the future, and why I must not see Judith, unaware of how often he repeated himself. I found it difficult to concentrate. I gazed at the photograph beneath his twitching fingers. It was a picture of a couple: A pretty girl, with a patterned shawl sliding from her shoulders, was hugging a young man. A little off-balance from her embrace, he was laughing and waving his hat. Except for the synagogue in the background, they might have been my parents in happier times.

"Your mother was a good woman," Tobias said. "Do you remember who your father was?"

"What do you mean?"

"Leave Judith alone. She's worth so much more than you."

Rather to my surprise, Judith continued to come see me. One thing led to another, and we kissed for the first time on the balcony. Judith possessed a sweet, addictive quality related less to her physique than to her personality. This was characterized by submissiveness that I found both intoxicating and, as the weeks went by, increasingly irritating. I would make love to her with an ironic brutality, secure in the knowledge that she would accommodate my every desire. At the close of the long afternoons, I would gaze, wide-eyed, upon her bruises as she staggered around in search of her stockings. Her passiveness made her remote and enigmatic.

I rarely slept well. Armies would march through my thoughts, their dreary tramping keeping time with my heartbeat. Memories of my father were resurfacing. He would carry me on his shoulders while his men herded civilians over frost-stiffened grasses. "The world is an engine," he would say, his breath billowing around my face, "an engine clogged with filth. We are simply cleaning the engine so that it will run smoothly."

One night, I woke with a start. The balcony was discernible through the threadbare curtains. Its metalwork twisted like barbed wire. The room was very quiet. The sounds of the traffic had a muffled, distant quality. Skeletal fingers slid between the curtains. I recognized my mother's hand. She leaned into the room. Her hair was matted, the birthmark staining her nose was black, and shreds of flesh dangled from her cheekbones: "If Ivan ever learns whose son you are . . ." I sat up, shouting. Judith pressed her cool palm to my face.

"Are you all right, Christian? Were you having a nightmare?"

I pushed her aside and approached the curtains. A shadow-filled fold was where the hand had been. "Someone was here."

"Impossible," Judith said. "We're three floors up."

"I saw her hand."

"You can't be serious."

"There's something strange about that balcony," I said.

"Strange? What do you mean?"

"Did anything happen here?"

"No, of course not."

"Did you and Tobias choose this room for me deliberately?"

"I don't understand, Christian. Please . . . I want to sleep."

While leaving my rooms in the morning, I almost stepped on old Klara who had been crouching at my door. She scuttled away, flopping down the stairs, like a black, tattered chicken. I paused before descending after her in the darkness. I thought myself safe, when, shrieking my name, she clamped her claws into my leg. I shrieked, too, kicking out wildly. Instantly released, I leapt down the remaining steps, three at a time, nearly collided with Tobias, and stumbled into the street. I crashed into the invalid soldier. We rolled together on the pavement. His face was red with laughter, tears streamed down his cheeks, and his whole body shook from head to stumps.

The story continues as Christian discovers the connection between his mother and Tobias, and eventually becomes one of the beggars . . .

*Author's note: Tobias comes from the Book of Tobias, one of the apocryphal books of the Old Testament, and represents the strict, paternal, vengeful aspects of the Jewish tradition. Judith is the softer, feminine, compromising aspect of the same. Lisoria is a fictional town, a composite of Prague, Budapest, or any town in eastern Europe.

Scenes

The essence of a great deal of things
vanishes
the very instant they are put into words:
Writing is trying to pin down
the unpindownable.
Therefore, a Real Work transcends the attempt.
It transcends trying to describe.
                    —Anne Marijn Koppen, Leaping Into the Void Writer

The Shifting Earth

Danielle Russel

HIS FEET ROTATED ON the rusted orange pedals, mimicking the motion of the clinking chain. He looked down at the fractured sidewalk and suspected the earth's plates were to blame for the broken slabs of concrete that showed ruddy tree roots breaking through. He imagined the earth moving around itself, shifting and causing concrete to separate. It seemed to him that the earth did this with people as well—moved them closer together and then further apart, closer and further, back and forward, as if it would never let them decide for themselves. His face rushed through air thick with the smell of red wine, stewed beef, and deep-fried potato chips. He pedaled over sundrenched tar that discharged a wet heat of dead skin and dust, which stuck to his face. This proof of people's existence clung to his skin, and he didn't want any of it.

The closer he got, the more he felt as though the bike were pulling him. He sped past trees and moist lawns, and bounced over broken concrete without looking down. He got closer and closer, until his bike was on its side in the grass and he was standing beside it, unsure of where to look.

They had been together for years. She glanced across the grass at him. She had just returned from a run, and ribbons of sweat ran down her face. Her black Lycra pants were damp and tight around her legs. Even from the footpath he could see the drops of salt glistening on her skin. He wanted to place his fingers on her face and feel each translucent ribbon as it slid down her nose.

He moved across the grass to her.

He stood in front of her now. He reached up and traced the sweat down her face until she rested her eyes on him. His hands moved over her ears and brushed through her hair. A damp warmth rose from her head and seeped into his fingers.

He opened his mouth but produced no sound. Her eyes narrowed at his unusual lack of words, and her glance dropped from his eyes to his nose, and from his nose to his lips.

He felt her coldness, and vertigo caught hold of him. His hands dropped, reaching out toward the ground, as if to connect with the only living thing that would receive his touch.

She turned and walked to the house.

And then, once again, the bottom of his rubber soles touched the rusted pedals. He reached up and pressed one hand to his eyes and thought only of her sweat on his fingers.

He turned the pedals over each other, trying not to wonder if he was encouraging the thick plates beneath him to drift.

Waiters and Roses

Julie Wornan

ON THE TOP FLOOR OF CENTRE *Pompidou stands an unusual exhibit. An enormous block of something that appears to be bluish ice contains, as though frozen within it, a perfect life-size replica of a tea room, complete with two waiters dressed impeccably in black waistcoats over long white aprons in the fashion of that romantic time, early 21st century Paris. There are no customers. On each table a red rose glows like a little lamp in the gloom. The oeuvre is striking for its realism.*

None of the museum staff can tell you the origin of the work. Some think it has been there since the museum was built. Some say there was once an actual tea room here and claim to have dined there in the old days, when everyone could afford the museum fee and you didn't have to be wealthy to enjoy a snack high above the city, looking down on a jumble of roofs and graffiti-covered walls.

The waiters—Jean-Pierre and Jean-Luc—are anxious to clear up and go home. It is nearly closing time, the last few customers have gone, and it has started to rain. Jean-Pierre, elegant, professional, holds a tray bearing the last coffee cups as he turns toward Jean-Luc to encourage him to hurry. Jean-Luc has his back to us. His head is slightly tilted; his thoughts are elsewhere. He is looking at the roses.

"Rose-Marie has left me," he blurts.

Jean-Pierre is surprised. His colleague never talks about himself. Is it the rain? The roses? Should he find some words of comfort?

"Hey—it will be okay," he says.

"No," says Jean-Luc, "It will never be okay." He stands there holding his tray, a white napkin draped over his left arm. "I left her alone too much, worked too many hours. Even with all the over-time, we couldn't afford the life she wanted."

Then he says the thing they have both been avoiding: "You know we're fired."

"Yeah, I know. They're closing this place down." Jean-Pierre's professionalism crumbles, his face drops, and he, too, stops in his tracks. The rain hammers down on the glass.

"Nobody's hiring," he says.

"No. Restaurants aren't getting customers. People can't afford to eat out these days."

"Remember when we started? Seems like only yesterday that I got this great job, and Rose-Marie . . ." For a moment Jean-Luc seems about to cry.

"Oh I believe in yesterday," Jean-Pierre sings softly in English. Jean-Luc joins in and tops it with "There's no tomorrow . . ."

"Today," says Jean-Luc, firmly. "We'll stop at today. With the roses."

The rain lashes against the walls. Faster, faster. Inside the tea room, time runs more and more slowly. And then it stops.

A museum guard is telling a visitor that there was indeed a tearoom here forty years ago. It was the inspiration for this very fine life-size sculpture.

Sunday Talks

Patricia Rareg

IT'S SUNDAY MORNING on the Quai de la Tournelle and Antoine is ready to sell his paintings. The sun is shining, and Antoine leans against the low embankment wall, chatting and smoking with Raymond, who sells books at the next stall.
Both men enjoy the view of Notre-Dame—the spire in the distance with the rooster on top, and the side of the cathedral with its circular stained-glass window cut right out of the stone.

A barge glides over the water. A man on the rear deck waves at them, and they hold up their coffee cups in response. Antoine stretches his arms, and an arguing couple catches his eye. The man is stout and wears a trench coat, while his wife has something haughty in her walk. Antoine notices her Dior suit and the determination in her step. The couple hesitates before stopping next to his corner.

"Have fun," whispers Raymond.

Antoine gets rid of his cigarette butt in an empty coffee cup, and throws it in the cardboard box he uses as a dustbin.

"Good morning Madame, Monsieur. How can I help you?" he says smiling. The man shrugs and turns away, while his wife studies the paintings. Neither of them utters a word. *Fantastic*, thinks Antoine.

"They're quite interesting, but I'm looking for something different," says the woman, holding a painting of Saint Sulpice in front of her.

"Different from what?" asks Antoine.

"All the paintings sold in Paris are the same," she replies. "They're all of the Eiffel Tower, Montmartre . . . any Paris monument, in fact," she adds putting down the painting.

"I beg your pardon," Antoine snaps. "These paintings are my own work. Some of us are real artists, Madame!"

"You're a painter?" she says, her right eyebrow raised in a perfectly plucked arch.

"Yes. I'm a part-time art teacher, but the rest of my day is spent working in my studio. I come here to sell my paintings," explains Antoine. He shouldn't be justifying himself to this woman, he thinks.

"I guess it's not easy to be an artist nowadays," she says, a frown digging a line down the middle of her forehead.

"So, are you interested in buying a painting or not?"

"I don't know," she says hesitating, "What do you think of this one, or maybe that one?" she asks, turning to her husband, who is busy checking his phone and doesn't respond. She looks at him, then rolls her eyes and tucks an imaginary lock of hair behind her ear.

"I don't care. It's up to you," he says finally, putting the phone back in his pocket. "Now hurry; Mass starts at eleven."

"I know, but I promised the children I'd buy them a real painting of Paris," she says, "They said it was better than a postcard. Such clever children."

"If this man has produced all of these paintings, just buy one," he says, glancing at his wristwatch.

Oh God, Antoine thinks. *Buy something and leave, or just go to a gallery.*

"Fifteen euros! For a painting off the street?" she says looking straight at him this time.

Antoine glances around, embarrassed. There aren't many people here yet, but a few passersby stop and stare. Two young joggers stretching against the wall are captivated. The girl whispers something to the boy and they laugh.

"It's a fair price Madame," Antoine replies.

"Well, do you at least provide a certificate for your paintings?" she asks, ignoring his tone. "Proof of authenticity, I mean."

Antoine can feel his face burning. Sunday morning is quiet; people are usually easy and friendly. "Of course I don't," he finally answers. "But I can send you one. Are you from Paris?"

"No. Bordeaux. Anyway, I don't know . . ." she says with a frown. "I guess you'll be here after Mass, so I might come back then."

"Oh, I'll definitely be here after Mass," he replies.

Antoine lights a cigarette and watches them leave.

Vignettes

What requires courage?
This.
This paper, blank paper.
This action of writing
each and every time.

—Pamela Haylock Combastet,
Leaping Into the Void Writer

Checking Out
Emily Seftel

To read a book for the first time is to make an acquaintance with a new friend; to read it for a second time is to meet an old one.

—Anonymous

ALL MY FRIENDS WERE THERE. I made my way across the room, greeting them: Ramona was a bit off-kilter since she had found out her mother was pregnant. And Jo looked awfully different after cutting her hair, although I heard she had sold it to a wig shop for a tidy sum. And was that Margaret? Hey, Margaret, it's me, Emily.

I moved along the shelves, head cocked to one side, smiling and nodding in recognition as I pulled out the occasional book. *Tom, you got that fence painted in record time. Laura, I heard you just moved into a little house. On the prairie, right? Nancy, how's it going? All that detective experience, and you still haven't figured out how to make Ned Nickerson kiss you? If you're not happy with him, I think the Hardy Boys are around here somewhere—they just wrapped up the Arctic Patrol Mystery.*

I hadn't thought of these people in years, but as a child, I'd spent countless hours in their worlds. And from the moment I stumbled across the surprisingly large children's literature section at the American Library of Paris, I was drawn back into my old web of relationships.

When I had first ventured into this section, I'd felt like an intruder. I was twenty-seven years old, completing my master's degree. The next-oldest person in the room was nine years old, completing fourth grade. She was browsing near the Ws, lips moving slightly as she read the titles, red backpack slung over her shoulder.

I wanted to reach past her to grab a copy of *Little Town on the Prairie*, but she stood in front of that shelf and clearly belonged in this room more than I did. After all, I wasn't in Paris to renew my childhood literary acquaintances. I was there as a graduate student, to expand my intellectual horizons and challenge my preconceived notions.

At first I tried to ignore the feeling of being pulled into the children's section, and focused on more "serious" books. I hadn't been a student in years, and I had a lot of catch-up to do, especially compared with the others in my master's program. They were all recent graduates from prestigious universities and were far more fluent in French than I was. They could read an essay by de Tocqueville or Zola during their métro rides. I needed two hours to read the same excerpt.

In classes, we analyzed Bourdieu's aesthetic gaze, and debated Foucault's analysis of power and punishment, but in my book bag, Derrida and Beverly Cleary jostled for space. Before leaving for my seminars, I took care to pack the correct book. I had nightmares of everyone opening their copies of Roland Barthes' *Fragments d'un discours amoreux* while I tried to pretend that I hadn't just pulled out my bright yellow paperback: *Ramona Quimby, Age 8.*

I kept going back to the children's section, feeling ashamed. But they helped me, these familiar stories. I didn't have to think; I could just immerse myself. When I checked out books, I would tuck copies of *Charlie and the Chocolate Factory* and *Harriet the Spy* into my pile of weightier tomes.

Charlie and Harriet didn't fit into the intellectual persona that I was trying to cultivate. I wanted to be someone who could participate in philosophical debates, opine on structuralism or the deconstructionists. In truth, I remained hazy on the fundamentals of these ideologies, although I did learn the name of Laura Ingalls's two plough horses (Sam and David).

One day, the children's librarian saw me browsing.

"My daughter loves reading," she said. "Are you looking for books for your children? I have some recommendations."

My mind raced. I suddenly felt exposed, embarrassed that these books were for me. I knew that this was absurd—why would the children's librarian care if I wanted to read young-adult literature? Still, faced with a sudden rush of shame, I stammered the first thing that came to mind:

"They're for my, um, niece. She's eight," I added, unnecessarily.

"How nice," said the librarian. "Does she live here?"

"No . . . just coming to visit. She loves reading, so I'm stocking up on books."

I do not, needless to say, have a niece. But I do have a bit of self-dignity, and the fact that I'd just lied to a children's librarian, of all people, was both humiliating and revealing. I didn't need to justify myself to this woman, but I realized I had become accustomed to dissimulation. I spent my days feigning comprehension, moving haltingly through my new life in Paris. In the classroom, I rarely joined discussions, trying to hide my fumbling ability in French. After seminars, I emailed questions to my professors, rather than asking in person, so that I could double-check my grammar. In the evenings, I declined my classmates' invitations to bars, and spent my evenings surrounded by dictionaries and flashcards.

The children's books, uncomplicated and relaxing, were the mental equivalent of a warm bath. I celebrated with Laura when Pa won the town spelling bee, successfully beating Mr. Foster by spelling "xanthophyll." I rooted for Laurie as he curled up next to Jo on the couch, trying to stop her from leaving. Why not spend time with them? It was certainly easier than deciphering Bourdieu's opinion of the historical genesis of a pure aesthetic.

The next time the librarian asked me if I needed help, I said no. This time, the books were for me.

Italian Bells

Claire Fallou

UNDER A SCORCHING SUN, the three of us climb through
a maze of soft-colored houses to the top of the hilly village of
Albagiara, in southern Italy. It is early afternoon and time for
a siesta: All shutters are drawn and there is no one in sight
except for a few cats stretched out lazily in white-hot spots
of Mediterranean light. Even in the narrow, shady alleys that
spring from sun-stricken little plazas the air is thick and quite
hard to breathe.

Everything would be still if it weren't for us. Peter,
dark-haired and stocky in a polo shirt and khaki shorts,
mumbles that it's too hot for such exercise and lags behind,
the soles of his tennis shoes rubbing with a squish against the
uneven pavers. Greg hops on ahead of us, his blond hair and thin
frame bobbing left and right. He does not mind the heat; he's so
full of curiosity and energy, he seldom minds any nuisance at

all. Sometimes he stops for a second, points an appreciative finger at a new object of interest—a pastel-coloured wall or the flaming purple tones of bougainvillea blossoms—then drops a few enthusiastic words and hurries toward the summit.

My limbs are heavy and my heart pounds hard, but I feel invigorated in my floating sundress. I notice new details at every twist and turn: a semi-circular marble fountain against a pink wall, a carved wooden door under a limestone lintel, a solemn line of dark-green cypress trees.

I have known my two companions for years. Peter is dating my best friend, Sandra, whom we have left down at a café with a cold drink and a book. We've traveled around Europe: There are pictures of us shopping in the rain on the windy streets of Notting Hill, soaking up pints in smoke-filled Berlin bars, riding a ramshackle, soot-blackened train between Belgrade and Sarajevo. This trip to Italy may be the last we do together in a long while; college is over and with all of us starting new jobs it may be some time before we can travel together again. I have signed a dry employment contract for a position in Paris, but I try to push back any thought of it.

Finally we are above the houses and bougainvilleas. We climb up a last rickety stairwell whose broken steps wobble and shriek under our weary feet. All that is here at the top of the hill is a naked patch of yellow grass with a tall, shadowless Jesus standing on a high pedestal of pale stone. His arms are open wide, his face soft and grave, as though to greet us with a solemn welcome.

The sun flares down, but the air circulates a little up here. I feel it caress my bare neck and shoulders; the light material of my sundress flutters gently around my legs. I feel as if I am whole again, no longer a perspiring mess of tired muscles and burning airways. The thick weeds rustle at our feet; they give off acid whiffs of dying grass that mingle with the sweet, earthy scents of fig trees and citrus flowers rising in the heat from the village below.

There are some benches at the foot of the statue; we crash down on them. I sigh, catch my breath and wipe a drop of sweat that is running down the side of my face. Peter shuts his eyes, leans back and lifts his face to the sun.

A condor gives a hoarse call; the weeds whisper softly.

From our spot the view opens onto the village. Far away to the west shines a stretch of sapphire sea. Below, nestled in the arms of some brownish mountains, is the tight-knit maze of houses we have just climbed through. I notice that some of them are old and wrinkled, and that time has dulled their colorful paint to dust: Canary yellows have become ochre, almond greens have turned dirty white, red tiles now show patches of gray. They exude a feeling of progressive abandon.

I feel I'm here doing exactly what I should: admiring the sunny world with my closest friends, enjoying my last days of youth and freedom before I start working in September. Whatever seconds of bliss I can gather before then I preserve in my heart: When my days are spent arranging nameless numbers on a bleak computer screen, I will let my mind fly back to this place and this moment.

Despite the heat, we stay there for some time, swapping jokes about which rusty hostel we're going to sleep in tonight. Then we fall quiet.

Down in the village the first bell starts to chime, shaking up the silence.

It wakes up a few others; they follow suit. Their metallic sounds go rolling through the air.

I close my eyes to count how many I can distinguish. I focus, and hear a fast peal of bronze ringing to the left, then a high-pitched, silvery melody rising from the right; and somewhere in between, two slow massive gongs beat different rhythms, one duller than the other. Four bells. Their songs cut through the heat with surprising sharpness. They mingle and overlap and intertwine and on rare occasions answer one another. The air vibrates now, filled with clear music and muffled echoes, and the empty sky teems with a rush of life.

Sitting on the bench, my eyes still closed, I picture the bells taking flight like a giant flock of black-and-white birds rising into the sky. I imagine I am one of them.

Stripes

Jean-Bernard Ponthus

IT IS THE BEGINNING of autumn in Paris and the morning air is cool and fresh.

While on the train commuting to the northwest suburbs this morning, I noticed a young man across the aisle wearing a hat with navy blue stripes. The hat was pulled tight on his head, covering his ears. As I looked at this man, I recalled that my friends have pointed out to me that I often wear stripes when casually dressed.

In the Middle Ages, stripes were synonymous with the Devil. A striped coat of arms was considered a token of ill omen, according to Michel Pastoureau, an expert on the symbolism of color.

Centuries later, when Betsy Ross stitched the first American flag, in 1776, the thirteen stripes represented the first colonies to rebel against the British monarchy.

In 1986, French contemporary artist Daniel Buren designed striped columns for the Palais-Royal as a tribute to this motif. His stark black and white columns sparked an intense debate over the combination of contemporary art and historic buildings.

I wonder why I often wear stripes.

Odes

Real Work looks at you and waits,
maybe for a really long time,
in the shadows,
to catch your eyes looking back—
un regard.

—Estefania Santacreu-Vasut,
Leaping Into the Void Writer

Under the Skin of Sylvia Plath

Manilee Sayada

I ENTER THE TINY ROOM that smells of humidity and glows in dark shades of yellow light.

This is the only bookshop in town where, in their spaces between book covers, words march, dance, laugh, eat, and sleep. When required, the words pose as still as mimes. The books here resist lining up like well-disciplined soldiers and are instead scattered in piles on counters and chairs, even on the floor.

I walk past an ancient water fountain that holds coins entrusted with travelers' dreams and up fragile, curvy stairs and enter a set of small rooms that hold secrets, sensations, and messages just for me.

I pick up a book and see a smiling Sylvia Plath sitting on the beach in a yellow bikini, exposing her naked, vulnerable skin on the cover of *Johnny Panic and the Bible of Dreams*. But no one ever panics in loneliness in this multi-room bookshop, not even Sylvia Plath in this photo. I open the book and read:

> *From where I sit, I figure the world is run by one thing and this one thing only. Panic with a dog-face, devil-face, hag-face, whore-face, panic in capital letters with no face at all—it's the same Johnny Panic, awake or asleep.*

Sylvia Plath did not shy away from the dark. In a time of despair, when the pain of rejection had grown in her bones, she wrote about this very feeling:

> *Nothing stinks like a pile of unpublished writings, which remark I guess shows I still don't have a pure motive (O-it's-such-fun-I-just-can't-stop-who-cares-if-it's-published-or-read) about writing. . . I still want to see it finally ritualized in print.*

She wrote, and wrote and wrote, until the century's coldest winter crept under her skin.

I imagine one night in London: Snow knocked against the windows and a bitter breeze snuck in through the gaps underneath the doors and windows. The kitchen counter of Sylvia's tiny flat was covered with dirty plates, pans and pots, and the remains of a roasted chicken with potatoes, carrots, and onions exuding a lingering smell of rosemary and garlic.

Sylvia sat her daughter next to her on the bed and held her son close to her heart and whispered, "O love, how did you get here? The pain you wake to is not yours . . ."

No one will ever know how long it took her to clear the mess, to wash the dishes clean of food and happiness. No one will ever know how many years, how many moments of despair, how many rejections it took to bring Sylvia to her very last moments of darkness. She may have stayed up all night before walking to the children's rooms to leave some cookies and milk, closing the door slowly, and then placing a towel under the door to make sure the gas would not leak out.

She closed the door, this poetess-genius, and turned on the gas oven, and waited for her death. Inside of one minute, the room became crowded by silence, darkness, rejection, disillusion, loneliness, and, finally—the end of this life spent in unceasing search for meaning—death.

Now, as I read, Sylvia Plath's words of self-doubt and questions that reveal her pain make the blood rush through my skin to tickle and move my fingers to write my own revelations, questions and secrets. Her honesty encourages me to expose my own humanity.

She even dared to look into her dreams, to consider the possibility they held a nothingness that could swallow her: Sylvia wrote about her one dream, what she called, "a dream of my dreams."

In this dream there's a great half-transparent lake stretching away in every direction, too big for me to see the shores of it, if there are any shores . . . At the bottom of the lake—so deep

I can only guess at the dark masses moving and heaving—are the real dragons . . .

These dragons are so large, Plath writes, that to call them enormous does not describe them. She depicts the dragons as having more wrinkles than even Johnny Panic. She cautions: *Dream about these long enough and your feet and hands shrivel away when you look at them too closely.*

I stand in the small room, listening to the sound of birdsong through an open window, the hush of book worshippers, and the sweet whispers of lovers in the corner.

I close my eyes and touch the dragon's wrinkle, and his enormous aging beauty takes me deep into the ocean where there is no space or need for panic.

Sylvia's dragons remind me that dragons live within my own body, under my own skin. I have always known they are there; I have seen them before but doubted their existence. Now I know I was not just imagining them because Sylvia saw them too. We have both seen how small our hands are next to their giant scales.

The passage of time has made me forget my own dragon dreams. Time, time, time: I spend it holding on to time itself, saving time, finding time, expanding time.

I walk down the stairs and out of the bookstore carrying Sylvia's words inside me.

Sylvia Plath (October 27, 1932 – February 11, 1963) was an American poet, novelist and short story writer. In the early morning of February 11, 1963, Plath took her own life. She placed her head in a gas oven after completely sealing the rooms between herself and her children. Plath wrote poetry from the age of eight, a poem that appeared in the Boston Traveller. By the time she arrived at Smith College she had written over fifty short stories and published in a raft of magazines. It is, however, her 1965 collection, Ariel, published posthumously, on which Plath's reputation essentially rests. In 1971, the volumes Winter Trees and Crossing the Water were published in the UK, including nine previously unseen poems from the original manuscript of Ariel. The Collected Poems, published in 1981, contained poetry written from 1956 until Plath's death. Plath was awarded the Pulitzer Prize for poetry, and became the first poet to win the prize posthumously. Sylvia Plath's gravesite in Yorkshire is now visited by hundreds of people each year. All excerpts from this piece are from her work.

Overlooked

Karen Isère

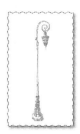

Warm is the air and balmy.

Light shimmering lonely, soon

To be repainted into September night.

Time draws its breath, shedding

Gold,

Chipping the days away, rehearsing

      Darkness.

I walk out, take a step and stop, caught.

Beyond the river lies Notre-Dame. Or rather, no,

She stands.

Her presence bearing massive on the island, yet she is sailing,

Whirling me windy,

Lifting.

A vertical journey where

Arches flow gracefully to statues and crosses and escalading peaks

All heading to the skies.

I breathe all in,

Though it is breathtaking.

The white stone and blue sky speak of silence.

But as a seagull paints a line across the trees, its cry startles me.

I land.

Noise pressing from all sides,

Voracious engines,

Car after car after bus after car,

And the odd horn, competing for attention,

While scooters wriggle free.

Hooting the past away,

Smothering

A present.

Rush hour, when cars can't rush but roar with spite.

The traffic light turns red.

From crawl to stop.

Japanese tourists, heels meeting pavement neatly. No looking back.

The site has been seen,

Done.

In their wondrous boxes the drivers have not budged.

Hands on wheels, they stare. Ahead.

If noses inched, a journey to the right, eyes would meet her, the Lady cathedral.

Very few muscles involved.

Were they born far away,

They would pay they would pray to be here,

They would jumbojet an ocean to see her.

But hands on wheels they stare ahead. Willing themselves away.

Held up. Intent.

On their way they are nowhere. Neither here nor there.

From A to B a mental tunnel. Should be smooth. Almost Mathematical.

The light is red, what a present,

Lavishing pearls of time.

Amidst the roar a new rhythm, a song ?

From up high the bells have woken,

Calling to a God all but dead,

Setting the hour but timeless, calling us now but heedless.

      Look up, look down, look 'round!

September time ticks 2011 away,

This hour still balmy, today

Lavishing seconds and twirling.

The light turns green,

The traffic glides westward.

Awful day and traffic on the way,

some will say.

Handmade to perfection, bearing eternity

She has been routined out, a powerless beauty?

At times I walk to her, close.

And puzzle as they gaze,

The saints and demons and angels and sinners and Jesuses and Marys and Gods.

All willed out of hope in ages we call Middle.
At times she shimmers from a distance
Whispering silence
Twin towers jeweled out against the sky
Though rock solid and rooted in the city
They could be smashed
So easily.
In an age that can kill eternity.

Dear George

Anna Pook

Dear George,

I've just put my six-month-old daughter, Maude, to bed. When she woke up crying I held her in my arms and hummed "Twinkle, Twinkle, Little Star" so the sound would reverberate in my chest and lull her to sleep. I breathed in the milky-sweet scent of her skin and let her peaceful, almost imperceptible sighs ease me into a state of serenity.

I'm sitting down at my desk to write to you. I want to say thank you.

Thank you for making me feel like a guest in your home rather than a customer in your bookshop: for providing a piano so that as my boyfriend, Dorian, waits for me to finish class, he can pick up a Bach concerto from your collection and play; for creating cushion-covered cubbyholes for me to curl up in and catch my breath; for letting me thumb through your books to my heart's content without the fear of an over-zealous bookseller frowning upon me.

We didn't know each other well, but as your daughter Sylvia once said: "To get to know him, you have to know the bookshop, because the two are the same, basically."

I know every inch of the upstairs library at Shakespeare and Company. I wonder if I got to know you.

In two weeks I will return there to resume my Evening Writing Workshops. During my pregnancy, as the participants regaled each other with their stories, discussed their dreams, forged friendships, and caught cookie crumbs in the pages of their notebooks, my baby would kick with delight, her feet hitting my ribs, making me squirm in my seat and pat my growing belly.

Over the years, you would often walk through the tiny book-filled library to your apartment. The participants' heads would be down as they scribbled enthusiastically in their notepads, occasionally stopping to laugh at their own discoveries, sigh over a newfound memory, or take a moment to gather their thoughts.

But I would see you, in your coat of many colors, patches of unpredictable purples, pinks and reds, your black Labrador, Colette, at your side. As you softly shuffled through the space, your face animated by its own story, your blue eyes glistened. In an instant you would disappear and leave me to only imagine you moving about in the bohemian dwelling that lay behind that door. You yourself seemed a figure of fiction. With your wispy white hair, you were Prospero and Merlin: a conjurer of dreams and a giver of gifts.

Your gift to me was allowing me to use your library for the workshop without asking anything in return—a token of pure generosity. When I make my way through the bookshop, past the fountain filled with the dreams of travelers, up the shoe-box stairs to the library, I am always reminded of this by the words of Yeats written in spindly black letters above the doorway:

Be not inhospitable to strangers, lest they be angels in disguise.

I am so looking forward to returning to your library. I always sit in the exact same spot, right opposite the window that overlooks Notre-Dame as it lights up green in the winter months, and frames the confetti-pink leaves of the cherry blossom trees in the spring. To my left, a *Great Gatsby* poster hangs in the corner of the room just above the ornate mirror with the golden frame. A glass-topped table convalesces under the window after its leg fell off and was replaced by a well-stacked pile of old books by the attending tumbleweeds. Above my head is the chandelier with one bulb that refuses to work. It casts a warm yellow glow that makes the participants squint after two hours of writing as they stretch out their weary fingers, arch their backs, and settle into satisfied smiles. If I reach down I can feel the ceramic of the terracotta floor tiles, whose cool exterior reassures my nerves as I pick up my notes and begin.

On that first night of class, we are a group of strangers, our shoulders slightly tensed, our hearts pumping loudly in our ears as we introduce ourselves, our eyes averted. But as the seven weeks roll by, I see each member of the group relax, their fingers no longer gripping their pens with fear, each voice a little louder as their stories begin to unfold, stretch out, and take shape. The room is filled with the sounds of laughter, the tap-tap of typing, and, if we're lucky, the scent of Nancy's homemade chocolate cookies.

While most shops are closing for the night, Shakespeare and Company still opens its doors, its arms, and welcomes the wondrous writers of Paris in from the cold. We sit in a circle, perched on the honey-colored wooden benches strewn with cushions, and for two hours we forget the outside world. Snuggled closely together as if around a campfire, we take turns to talk, share, and write.

It was Erin who told me of your death in an email simply entitled "George."

I hadn't seen you for months, maybe even a year but I felt your presence in every nook and cranny of that library, in every page of your much-loved books. In death, you became real once more, not a figment of my imagination, not a character in a book that I can go back to time and time again, not a magician but a humble human being.

One who taught me that stories are there to be shared.

Your legacy lies not only in the bricks and stones of the building so many call home. It lies in the gestures of generosity that germinate right there in the library: in the covert conversations between participants as they collaborate on a homemade children's story for Maude after class; in the breaking of Nancy's cinnamon bread; in Martin's passing 'round a paper bag of peanuts, each one permeated with precious memories of his nostalgic trip home to Detroit; in Karen's polished performance of a scene from James's screenplay acted out in the center of the space.

As I sit in that space once again this winter, I will think of you passing through, reaching down to pat Colette, and I will miss you.

With love and respect,

Anna

Biographical Notes

EDITORS:

Erin Byrne writes travel essays, poetry, fiction and screenplays, and is the author of *Wings: Gifts of Art, Life, and Travel in France* (Travelers' Tales, 2016), editor of *Vignettes & Postcards From Morocco* (Reputation Books, 2016), and writer of "The Storykeeper" film. Her work has won three Grand Prize Solas Awards for Travel Story of the Year, the Readers' Favorite Award, Foreword Reviews Book of the Year Finalist, and an Accolade Award for film. She is an occasional guest instructor at Shakespeare and Company and teaches on Deep Travel trips. Her screenplay, *Siesta,* is in pre-production in Spain, and she is working on the novel, *The Red Notebook.* www.e-byrne.com.

Anna Pook grew up in South London and originally trained as a performer, specialising in Musical Theatre at the BRIT School, and graduating from the University of Brighton with a BA in Theatre and Visual Art. An experienced teacher, she has worked in the UK, India and France. From 2009 to 2014, she was the resident creative writing instructor at the Shakespeare and Company.

Anna pursued her MA in Prose Fiction from the University of East Anglia, where she was the 2014/15 recipient of the Man Booker Scholarship. She is currently working on her debut novel.

PHOTOGRAPHERS AND ARTISTS:

William Curtis Rolf is a photographer whose life-long affection for European lifestyles of the 17th, 18th and 19th centuries brings a sense of elegance and gentility to his imagery. His photographic sensibility is sought after by collectors, designers and art directors throughout the globe. His fine art prints, as well as his books, are in the private collections of individuals whose own homes and offices reflect that same interest and affection.

After earning a BA in English Literature from UCLA then graduating first in his class from ArtCenter College of Design in photography, William started shooting ads for a number of Fortune 500 clients. But it was during his stint as Creative Director of Photography at E&J Gallo Winery that he developed many of his complex photo production skills. He not only personally shot most of their principal location and studio assignments, he also oversaw a staff of four photographers as well as a large support staff. It was there that he gained the focused managerial and communication skills that serve him today.

Since 1997 William has been focusing his efforts on fine art photography projects and related books.

Colette Hannahan is a San Francisco-based painter and writer. Her work is about the simple moments of beauty and magic that stop her in her tracks. She starts her paintings with a slice of architecture or landscape, then builds up layers of color and glaze until the fog rolls in and the light spins through the open sky. Colette has painted and exhibited around the Bay Area and in France, and her writing has appeared in Geographic Expeditions' *Wanderlust.* She was recently a featured reader at the award-winning San Francisco travel writing series, Weekday Wanderlust. Her website is colettehannahan.com.

Candace Rose Rardon is a writer and artist whose stories and sketches have appeared on sites such as BBC Travel's Words & Wanderlust column, AOL Travel, World Hum, Gadling, and National Geographic Traveler's Intelligent Travel blog. Her travel blog, The Great Affair, has been featured in *The New York Times.*

Nicholas Adamski is Co-Executive Director of The Poetry Society of New York, Co-Curator/Director of Operations at The Poetry Brothel, and Co-Founder of the New York Poetry Festival.

Christina Ammon has penned stories on a wide range of topics, from flying with raptors in Nepal to exploring the underground wine scene in Morocco. She received the Oregon Literary Arts

Fellowship for Creative Nonfiction, and her articles and photos have appeared in *Conde Nast, Hemispheres, The San Francisco Chronicle, The L.A. Times, The Oregonian* and many other publications. Christina designs and leads Deep Travel Trips, most recently to Nepal and Morocco. www.vanabonds.com.

David Barnes lives above a noisy bar in the Bastille neighbourhood of Paris with his cat, Toast. He edited the prose in the anthology *Strangers in Paris* (Tightrope Books, 2011) and has published poems and short stories. He works as a gestalt psychotherapist. David hosts the reading series SpokenWord Paris, runs writing workshops at Shakespeare & Company bookstore and edits the literary journal *The Bastille*. He once had transient global amnesia. He grew up in the Oxfordshire village where Agatha Christie is buried. Reachable at spokenwordparis.org.

Maria Bitarello is a Brazilian writer, journalist, translator, photographer and filmmaker. She speaks four languages and was formerly based in Paris. Her writing is found on her blog (http://ioncemetagirl.com) and also on websites for the Parisian folk band Clint is Gone, African photo exhibition *Iya Shango* and Brazilian documentary film *Silence 63*. Maria has published academic papers, book reviews and columns in Portuguese, and has also contributed to the research and writing of a Brazilian book on aviator Santos Dumont, *Santos Dumont: retorno às origens*, San Antonio Studios, 2007. In 2010, she was International Associate Editor for *XXXIX Mester*, a publication of the Department of Spanish and Portuguese at the University of California, Los Angeles (UCLA) and in 2011 her band from Brazil had its first self-titled EP, *duplodeck,* released by Pug Records.

Kate Buljanovic writes short stories and travel essays. She has travelled extensively in Africa and Europe. Kate grew up in Johannesburg, South Africa and completed a master's program in European studies in Zagreb, Croatia. She has written a travel piece entitled *A Pinch of Sali,* about a village festival on the island of Dugi Otok, Croatia, and her story *The Chair* is about the comforting aspect of place.

Kimberley Cameron has been a literary agent for twenty-five years. She recently sold Senator Barbara Boxer's memoir, *The Art of Tough* to Hachette, and has started the careers of many debut authors. She co-founded Knightsbridge Publishing Company with offices in New York and Los Angeles. In 1993 she became partners with Dorris Halsey of The Reece Halsey Agency, founded in 1957. Among its clients have been Aldous Huxley, William Faulkner, Upton Sinclair, and Henry Miller. She opened Reece Halsey North in 1995 and 2009 the agency became Kimberley Cameron & Associates. She now has several agents working with her agency. She resides and works from Tiburon, California and France, with many visits to New York to make the rounds of editorial offices.

She is interested in writing that makes a reader feel something, whether it be fiction or non-fiction. Some of the genres she particularly enjoys are mystery and crime, thriller, science fiction, women's fiction, horror and literary fiction.

Non-fiction genres are health, science, biography, memoir and history.

Sana Chebaro was born and raised in England and is of Lebanese origin. She writes about her cultural and travel experiences, from expositions or pizzas in Paris to adventures in Burma, Cuba and Venezuela. Her work has appeared in *Airways Magazine.* Sana is currently working on *Under the Lilac Tree*, a collection of short stories which explores multiple themes of migration, broken marriages, identity and repatriation. Sana currently lives in Paris with her husband. Her work can be found on: sanachebaro.blogspot.com.

Billy Collins is the author of 12 collections of poetry, most recently *Aimless Love: New and Selected Poems* (Random House, 2013). He also edited the poetry anthologies *Poetry 180: A Turning Back to Poetry, 180 More: Extraordinary Poems for Every Day,* and *Bright Wings: An Anthology of Poems about Birds* (with David Sibley). He is a Distinguished Professor at Lehman College (CUNY) and a Fellow of the Rollins Winter Park Institute. He served as United States poet laureate (2001-2003).

Janis Cooke Newman is the author of the recently released novel, *A Master Plan for Rescue,* as well as the historical novel, *Mary; Mrs. A. Lincoln,* and the memoir, *The Russian Word for Snow.* She is the founder of the Lit Camp writers conference.

Marcia DeSanctis is the *New York Times* bestselling author of *100 Places in France Every Woman Should Go* (Travelers' Tales, 2014). She is a former television news producer who has worked for Barbara Walters, ABC, CBS, and NBC News. Her work has appeared in *Vogue, Marie Claire, Town & Country, O the Oprah Magazine, National Geographic Traveler, More, Tin House,* and *The New York Times,* and other publications. She is the recipient of four Lowell Thomas Awards for excellence in travel journalism, including one for Travel Journalist of the Year for her essays from Rwanda, Haiti, France and Russia.

Ann Dufaux taught for many years at Centre de Linguistique Appliquée, Université de Franche Comté in Besançon, France. She writes fiction, travel stories, and poetry. Her work has been long-listed for Ireland's Fish Publishing Prize. She enjoys meeting people and learning languages in places around the world such as Vietnam, Greece, Tunisia, Mexico and Nicaragua. Ann is the mother of four, and enjoys reading, singing and Tai Chi. She and her husband recently completed 2,000 km on the Compostela Trail.

Anna Elkins is a traveling poet and painter. She earned a BA in Art and English and an MFA and Fulbright Fellowship in Poetry. Her writings have been published in journals and books, and her paintings hang on walls around the world. She has written, painted, and taught on six continents. She is the author of the illustrated vignette, *The Heart Takes Flight,* the novel *The Honeylicker Angel,* and the poetry collection *The Space Between.* She also illustrated the books *Wings: Gifts of Art, Life,* *and Travel in France* and *Vignettes & Postcards Morocco*. Anna has set up her easel and writing desk in the mythical State of Jefferson. www.annaelkins.com

Claire Fallou writes articles, creative non-fiction pieces and personal essays on travel, culture and the economy. Her work has appeared in the *Financial Times, La Tribune, Paris Revisited*, and Grand Ecart, a website dedicated to cinema for which she covered the Cannes Film Festival in spring 2015. In 2011, Claire won the *Financial Times/The Economist* Nico Colchester Award for aspiring journalists. Claire lives in Paris.

Jennifer Flueckiger writes essays and short stories that explore the humorous side of traveling, cultural exchanges, sport and everyday life. She has been published in UK literary magazine, *Mslexia*, and her blog, theaccidentalparisienne.wordpress.com. Jennifer is currently working on *McSoccer for Girls*, a memoir about her experience coaching girl's football/soccer in Scotland. Jennifer was born and bred in the US and lived in Scotland for twenty years. She currently lives in Scotland. To find out more about Jennifer, see jenniferflueckiger.com.

Don George is the author of the bestselling books *The Way of Wanderlust* and *Lonely Planet's Guide to Travel Writing*. In a quarter-century of adventuring, Don has been Global Travel Editor for Lonely Planet and Travel Editor for the *San Francisco Examiner* and *Chronicle*, and for Salon.com, where he founded the award-winning Wanderlust site. Don is currently Editor at Large for *National Geographic Traveler* and Special Features

Editor for BBC Travel. Don teaches and lectures around the world on travel and travel writing, and is the co-founder and chairman of the acclaimed annual Book Passage Travel Writers and Photographers Conference.

Catalina Girón was born and raised in Santiago, Chile. She discovered the world of writing at the age of nine when her godmother gave her a blue notebook and a five-color pen. She lived in San Diego and New York City, where she wrote her memories of being a college student expat. With a strong sense of humor and sometimes tri-lingual confusion among Spanish, English and French, Catalina weaves words to relate her experiences of culture and the bizarre. Catalina currently lives in Paris, and is working on a project that combines her two passions for literature and visual aesthetics. To find out more about her, you can visit her blog noviaenparis.wordpress.com.

Georgia I. Hesse, founding travel editor of Hearst's *San Francisco Examiner*, freelance writer, editorial consultant, photographer, writing instructor and lecturer, was born on the 28 Ranch, Crazy Woman Creek, Wyoming. A BA graduate from Carleton College, Northfield, Minnesota, she studied political science on a Fulbright scholarship at Paris' Sorbonne and the University of Strasbourg in Alsace. Georgia holds the *Ordre de la République* from the French government and the *Chevalier l'Ordre de la République* from Tunisia. She is author of guidebooks to France and Paris, to San Francisco and Northern California published by Fisher, Penguin, and Berlitz.

Karen Isère is a Franco-British journalist and photographer based in Paris. Her features are mostly published by the magazines *Paris Match, Psychologies Magazine* and *Le Monde des Ados*. After specializing in health and psychology journalism, Karen has moved into international coverage, such as the Chechen conflicts and the situation of Christians in the Middle East. She worked with the internationally acclaimed Brazilian photographer Sebastiao Salgado on his Genesis project, which encompassed eight years around the world showing people and places yet untouched by the modern world. Karen also writes weekly literary reviews for the magazine *Télé7Jours*, poetry, travel stories and flash fiction, both in English and French.

Catherine Karnow, the daughter of journalist Stanley Karnow, was born and raised in Hong Kong, and graduated from Brown University with honors degrees in Comparative Literature and Semiotics. Her work appears in *National Geographic, National Geographic Traveler, Smithsonian,* French *GEO* and many other international books and magazines. Her retrospective: *Vietnam: 25 Years Documenting a Changing Country* opened at the Art Vietnam gallery in Hanoi in April 2015. Catherine is also a passionate photography educator. She is based in San Francisco, and gives private workshops and teaching seminars all over the world, for *National Geographic,* as well as her own signature workshops in Umbria and Vietnam. www. catherinekarnowphotoworkshop.com

Leslie Lemons grew up in Texas and New Mexico and received a master's degree in social work administration from the

University of Michigan. Her love of writing evolved through twenty years in the nonprofit sector as she wrote articles, grants, newsletters and marketing materials to raise funds and awareness for causes including culture and the arts, healthcare, at-risk youth, education and child abuse prevention. Leslie lives in Normandy, France with her husband, and is currently working on *Redemption in the Redlands,* a memoir based on the events of an infamous shoot-out in a small East Texas town in the early 1930's, resulting in the tragic deaths of three of her relatives.

Kimberley Lovato is a writer, traveler, and Champagne drinker whose articles and essays have appeared in magazines and websites such as *National Geographic Traveler, American Way, Celebrated Living, Delta Sky, Every Day With Rachel Ray, Virginia Living,* the *San Francisco Chronicle*, BBC. com, travelandleisure.com, and many more. Her book, *Walnut Wine & Truffle Groves*, about the people and food of the Dordogne region of France, was the Lowell Thomas Award-winning book of 2012, and her personal essays have appeared in volumes 8, 9 and 10 of *The Best Women's Travel Writing* and have also received recognition from Travelers' Tales Solas Awards. Read more about her at www.kimberleylovato.com.

Laura Mandel is a creative non-fiction writer who focuses on themes of family, relationships, travel and culture. She has a degree in creative writing from the University of Pennsylvania.

Laura currently works in international content syndication for *The New York Times* in Paris.

Amy Marcott writes fiction and non-fiction. Her work has appeared in *Salt Hill, DIAGRAM, Necessary Fiction, Memorious, Juked*, and elsewhere. She has earned fellowships from the Virginia Center for the Creative Arts and the Somerville Arts Council as well as a scholarship to the Sewanee Writers' Conference. Her work has been nominated for a Pushcart Prize and awarded in *Glimmer Train's* Very Short Fiction Contest, among other honors. She currently resides in the Bay Area, where she's at work on a novel and is a member of the Lit Camp Board of Directors. www.amymarcott.com

Rosemary Milne is a writer whose career began in the 1970s when she co-wrote and edited the *Collins Robert French Dictionary*. She then spent ten years as a contributing editor to *Scottish Child* magazine. Her most recent non-fiction book is *Northern Lights, Building Better Childhoods in Norway* (2007), which she co-authored with Bronwen Cohen. Since her retirement she has entertained readers with her online Paris bulletins. Rosemary was born in Yorkshire and now divides her time between Paris and Scotland. She has published one novel, *The Twisted Yarn*, and is working on a second.

Jayme Moye, a compulsive storyteller, has written hundreds of travel narratives for more than fifty publishers including *Travel + Leisure, National Geographic Traveler, New York, Outside, Men's Journal, Women's Health*, and *Fodor's Travel*

Intelligence. In 2014, Jayme's essay "The Road Not Ridden," about a trip to Afghanistan to report on the country's first women's cycling team for ESPN, was anthologized in *The Best Women's Travel Writing, Volume 10.* That same year, the North American Travel Journalists Association named her Travel Journalist of the Year. When not traveling, Jayme splits time between Boulder, Colorado, and an island in Quebec.

Philip Murray-Lawson was born in Scotland, but has lived most of his adult life in Turkey and France. After taking an Honours degree in History at Aberdeen, Scotland, Philip became a teacher of EFL. He now runs Evolution-abc, a Paris based language consulting company: evolution-abc.com. His first publications focused on language training and appeared in *Prism, A Learning Journal.* Philip's first literary works were translations of two stories by the French *fin de siècle* writer Marcel Schwob. These appeared in *Udolpho*, the periodical of the Gothic Society to which he also contributed non-fiction articles. Philip's collection of horror stories, *Heresies,* was published in 2000. The writing workshops at Shakespeare and Company have encouraged his penchant for humorous horror stories. He was in the top ten in the Women On Writing Spring 2011 Flash Fiction contest and was interviewed on their blog, The Muffin.

Gonzague Pichelin is a French filmmaker who has directed and edited films in Europe, Africa and the US. He was co-director and cinematographer for the documentary *Les Funamblules de la mer* (France 3 and Planète Thalassa, 2015), and a short film about torture centers in Syria (Human Rights Watch, 2012). Gonzague was director of *Le lien à l'autre* (France, 2013), *Paroles de femmes au travail*, a documentary about workplace discrimination (France, 2010), and *Portrait of a Bookstore as an Old Man* (France 2003), broadcast in many places including the Sundance Channel. As cameraman, Gonzague has filmed two documentaries about the life of Venetians for Russian director Tatiana Danilyantz: *Hidden Garden* (Venice Film Meeting, 2008) and *Venice Afloat* (RTR Planeta, 2001 Yerevan International Film Festival, 2012). He has also edited several documentaries, and taught film in Parisian journalism schools, including l'Institut des Médias. As a writer, Gonzague has written an encyclopedia about vernacular architecture and construction techniques, and his book about immigrant entrepreneurs, *Boss Made in France*, (Editéa, 2009) received the Advancia Award from the Chamber of Commerce and Industry of Paris.

Jean-Bernard Ponthus has been writing articles for the internal newspaper at La Poste, *Société des Amis du Musée de La Poste*, for ten years and has been a curator of this museum. His articles deal with the cultural aspect of stamps, exhibitions sponsored by La Poste or reportage in the post offices of Paris, and his main exhibition was a private collection of the correspondence of Colette. He is currently creating a blog about the cultural life of Paris that focuses mainly on paintings. Jean-Bernard is also trained in photography and has edited postcards of Parisian urban landscapes. His photography blog can be found at broceliande1.unblog.fr. In 2014, Jean-Bernard was knighted in Arts and Letters by the French government.

Martin Raim is a long-serving and dedicated member of the Evening Writing Workshop who recently led several well-received sessions on topics ranging from Narrative Voice to Point of View. His short story "The Cell" was published in *Something Else*, Scott, Foresman and Co. 1970 and again under the title, "The Cage," in *Sudden Twists*, Jamestown Publishers, 1980. "Between the Doors" recently appeared in *Upstairs at Duroc*, an international literary journal published in Paris. Most recently, his work was shortlisted for the 2010 Paris Short Fiction Prize. American by birth, Martin has lived in France for twenty-two years and is currently working on a collection of creative non-fiction stories that sprung from his experience in the workshop at Shakespeare and Company.

Patricia Rareg was born in Martinique, and has a master's degree in British civilizations. Her short stories have been published in French in the *Eclosions* anthology, which was the combined work of the university Paris XII and AETP (Association of Writers and Professional Translators). Her first novel *"C'est l'heure!"* (The Time Has Come), was published in 2006. She has completed a second novel about dual personalities, betrayal and murder. Patricia is currently working on her third novel about a couple on holiday in a small village who hear strange noises during the night. She lives in Paris.

Alberto Rigettini, Italian, is a poet, playwright, screenwriter, poetry pimp and freak-show barker. He is host of "SpokenWord Paris," the fight club "Writers Get Violent" and "Le Bordel De la Poésie," The Poetry Brothel in Paris." He has been awarded The Lorca in Translation Competition, the Troubadour International Poetry Prize and his writing is included in the anthology *Strangers in Paris: New Writing Inspired by the City of Light.* He is currently writing a poetry collection in five settings: London, Spain, Italy, US and France.

Danielle Russel writes about the intricacies and intimacies of relationships. Born in New Zealand, she studied creative writing at the University of Auckland. Her fiction has appeared in *Spectrum 5*, a fifth edition anthology showcasing Auckland based writers. Danielle is currently working on her first novel, *So You Will Not Believe Something That Isn't True.*

Manilee Sayada studied comparative literature and music at the University of California Berkeley with some of the most renowned artists, writers and thinkers such as Trinh-T-Minh-ha, Robert Hass, June Jordan, Sharnush Parsipur and Judith Butler. She earned a master's degree in social sciences at the London School of Economics and Political Sciences. Currently, she works as an education consultant and a teacher in Paris.

Emily Seftel is a former Features reporter for the *Arizona Republic* whose work includes stories about the Jewish quarter of Los Angeles, off-Strip entertainment in Vegas and travel throughout Arizona. She has also written about her international misadventures, including an overnight hike up Mount Fuji, a slippery massage in Laos, and a short stint in a Slovakian holding cell. A native of Phoenix, Arizona, Emily lives in Paris with her husband, and is currently working on *French Lessons*, a collection of short stories about her life in Paris.

David Leo Sirois is a dual citizen of Canada and the US living in Paris. His poems appear in Anglophone Parisian magazines *THE BASTILLE, Belleville Park Pages*, and *Paris Lit Up*, as well as the French online journal *Terre à Ciel*, where his poem "CONTAINER" appears both in English and in French translation. His work was anthologized in the UK in *The Keystone Anthology*, and in the US in *Becoming Fire*. His first book, *Silver Shiver Fragment* (twenty-one years' work) will be published by SpokenWord Paris. *Songs to Growing Things*, split between poems to plants and to pigeons, is forthcoming.

Benjamin Sutherland, a reporter on retainer with *The Economist*, the newsweekly, lives between Santa Barbara, California, and Paris. He teaches undergraduate and graduate classes in geopolitics and narrative structure at schools in and near Paris including ISCPA, the Paris School of Business, and HEC, a university serially ranked Europe's top MBA program by *The Financial Times*. A former staff screenwriter for Cinemarket, a Paris production company, Sutherland also co-directed, with filmmaker Gonzague Pichelin, the award-winning Sundance Channel documentary *Portrait of a Bookstore as an Old Man*. He was head of reporting at *COLORS* magazine and later wrote for *Newsweek*.

Nancy Szczepanski writes about her experiences with food and travel. She has written about how she, the granddaughter of a butcher and the daughter of a sausage maker, became vegetarian, and how three years in Poland left her vowing to never again touch another spud. Nancy spent seven years in Japan where she came to love all manner of tofu: pure white and satiny *kinugoshi* tofu, slightly sweet, black speckled sesame or goma tofu, and her particular favorite, a tofu byproduct called yuba, made from the wrinkly skin that forms on top of soy milk. Nancy currently lives in Paris (France, not Texas) where she is creating a food blog.

Jane Weston Vauclair and her husband, David Vauclair, are the authors of *De Charlie Hebdo: À #Charlie: Enjeux, Histoire, Perspectives*. She recently completed a PhD on French satirical journalism from 1960 to 1970, which examined how the publications *Hara-Kiri* and *Charlie Hebdo* used provocative humour and parody to critique consumer culture in France. Jane teaches British history and literature at Paris Diderot University, and works as a translator. She has translated books on art history and the history of a hotel in Switzerland, and regularly translates academic articles in the social sciences, particularly development studies, with publishers including Oxford University Press and Le Livre d'Art. Besides her love of fiction, she is passionate about film and is a regular contributor of cinema critiques to *Franglaisreview*.

Julie Wornan a retired computer programmer, now enjoys the challenge of writing for humans instead of machines. She specializes in short speculative fiction, often using unusual takes on the natural and supernatural world to focus on real social and psychological problems. Julie's illustrated novel, *Let's Save Our Planet* (and its French version, *Sauvons la Planète*), helps young people understand climate change and related issues. She has had a number of stories and poems published on the websites Bewildering Stories and AntipodeanSF. Her most recently published works, *Grandpa's Book*, and *Black Cat in a Garden*, had their origin at Shakespeare and Company. Julie's hobbies include digital photography and graphic composition. You can see her imagery on flickr.com/photos/julieeiluj. A native New Yorker, she now makes her home in France.

Permissions

"*La Bonne Vie* in Paris" by Don George published with permission from the author. Originally published in the November 2012 issue of *National Geographic Traveler.* Copyright © 2012 by Don George.

"Twenty Years and Counting" by Marcia DeSanctis published with permission from the author. Originally published as "A Grand Return" in *Town & Country Weddings*, Fall/Winter 2011. Copyright © 2011 by Marcia DeSanctis.

"Mouffetard: Of Markets and Meandering" by Georgia I. Hesse published with permission from the author. Copyright © 2016 by Georgia I. Hesse.

"*Parfumerie*" by Anna Elkins published with permission from the author. Copyright © 2015 by Anna Elkins

"Oranges in Paris" by Benjamin Sutherland published with permission from the author. Copyright © 2015 by Benjamin Sutherland.

published in *The Bastille #3*, on July 2014, with the title: "Rarely Travel Unarmed."

"*Quatre Poèmes sur les Pigeons*" by David Leo Sirois published with permission from the author. Copyright © 2015 by David Leo Sirois.

"Travel by Train" by David Barnes published with permission from the author. Copyright © 2015 by David Barnes.

"Waking up in Notre-Dame" by Christina Ammon published with permission from the author. Copyright © 2015 by Christina Ammon.

"Word Embers" by Amy Marcott published with permission from the author. Copyright © 2015 by Amy Marcott.

"Inside the Lie of Paris" (excerpt from *A Master Plan for Rescue*) by Janis Cooke Newman published with permission from the author. Copyright © 2015 by Janis Cooke Newman.

"January in Paris" from *Ballistics: Poems* by Billy Collins, copyright © 2008 by Billy Collins. Used by permission of Random House, an imprint and division of Penguin Random House LLC. All rights reserved.

"Interview with Gonzague Pichelin, Filmmaker: *Portrait of a Bookstore as an Old Man* and Love Letters Project" by Erin Byrne published with permission from the author. Copyright © 2015 by Erin Byrne.

Photography and Art Credits

Cover—William Curtis Rolf

Map of Paris—Colette Hannahan

Stamp Sketches—Colette Hannahan

Nouveau—William Curtis Rolf

La Bonne Vie—William Curtis Rolf

Poetics—William Curtis Rolf

Paris, *je t'aime*—Candace Rose Rardon

Perspectives—William Curtis Rolf

The Top-Hatted SpokenWord Poets of Paris—Sabine Dundure

Illuminations—William Curtis Rolf

Portraits—Candace Rose Rardon

Vignettes & Postcards—William Curtis Rolf

Inspiration—William Curtis Rolf

Postcards—Candace Rose Rardon

Visions—William Curtis Rolf

Memory—William Curtis Rolf

Mystery—Candace Rose Rardon

Duende—William Curtis Rolf

Scenes—William Curtis Rolf

Vignettes—William Curtis Rolf

Odes—William Curtis Rolf

Reputation Books

CPSIA information can be obtained
at www.ICGtesting.com
Printed in the USA
FFOW04n0444190816
26786FF